Strand 5/00

Dance for *the* Land

Also by Clemence McLaren

Inside the Walls of Troy

Dance for the Land

by
Clemence McLaren

Atheneum Books for Young Readers

Acknowledgments

I thank my family and my writing group for their input and aloha *and my students at the Kamehameha Schools for constructive criticism on the manuscript and corrections of both Pidgin English and Hawaiian-language dialogue.*

Atheneum Books for Young Readers
An imprint of Simon & Schuster Children's Publishing Division
1230 Avenue of the Americas
New York, New York 10020

Book design by Nina Barnett
The text of this book is set in Janson Text.
Printed in the United States of America
10 9 8 7 6 5 4 3 2 1

Library of Congress Cataloging-in-Publication Data
McLaren, Clemence.
Dance for the land / by Clemence McLaren.—1st ed.
p.   cm.
Summary: When twelve-year-old Kate, who is half-white, moves to Hawaii with her brother and father, she becomes a victim of racial prejudice but also learns the meaning of her middle name.
ISBN 0-689-82393-2
1. Hawaii—Fiction. 2. Moving, Household—Fiction. 3. Prejudices—Fiction. 4. Family life—Fiction. I. Title.
PZ7.M2235Dan   1999   [Fic]—dc21   98-33761

FIRST
EDITION

To Olga Mākole Kaleinani Kalama,
who taught us hula and love.
And to my granddaughter, Kelsi Mahinalani Cottrell,
a child of the Islands.

Chapter 1

*T*he day had arrived—the day, hour, and minute Kate had been having nightmares about for months. She was about to leave the house she loved in Pasadena, California, for a place she didn't even like. And she was leaving behind her dog, Boggs. He wouldn't be welcome in their new home, a small apartment in a high-rise building in Honolulu, Hawai'i. They'd arranged for Kate's best friend, Sara Lindsey, to take him.

Now, with the house empty of furniture and a mound of suitcases in the front hallway, the Lindseys had come to pick him up. Boggs was looking up at them, jaws drooping with dog depression. Boggs knew. Instinctively, he knew something terrible was happening.

Meanwhile, the four people standing around in the bare living room were all pretending something terrible wasn't happening. But Sara Lindsey couldn't look Kate in the eye, and Sara's mother was holding the leash limply in her palm, as if she couldn't decide whether or not to drop it and go home.

Kate's father was a lawyer who knew how to put a positive slant on things. He was making a case for the wonderful new home Boggs was getting. "You'll have your own private dock," he was saying to the dog, "and your own lake to swim in."

Like all Labrador retrievers, Boggs loved to swim, and the Lindseys owned a weekend house on Lake Arrowhead. Kate eyed Mrs. Lindsey, who looked, as usual, like a model in a designer fashion catalog. She wondered if she could tell her that Boggs liked to play in the mud whenever he went swimming. She tried to picture Boggs rubbing his muddy flank against Mrs. Lindsey's immaculate white slacks. She tried to imagine what it would be like coming home from school in a strange city without her dog waiting for her, wagging his tail.

Kate wished the two adults would stop talking. Mrs. Lindsey was saying how much she admired Kate's father because he was going back home to work for the Hawaiians. She called them "your people." She said it was "wonderfully exciting" that the Kaheles were moving to Hawai'i, which she called "the Islands."

Sara reached down to pet the dog. "Honolulu, Waikīkī Beach. Lucky you," she murmured without looking up.

Kate pictured the rain-soaked jungle where her father's relatives lived. She wished Sara could see the weather-beaten bungalows and abandoned, rusting cars with vines snaking in and out of the windows. A lot of Hawai'i didn't look anything like Waikīkī Beach.

But Kate had explained all that. Sara knew this move was a disaster. She knew what it meant that they'd both graduated to pink satin toe shoes, that their ballet troupe was performing Sundays at the Los Angeles Museum Theater. In next season's *Nutcracker*, Kate would have had a good chance at the role of Sugar Plum Fairy. At the private school they both attended, Kate was going to miss the spring trip. And each one of them was losing a best friend.

Sara always talked when she got nervous. She probably couldn't think of anything else to say. Still, Kate was having a hard time feeling sorry for her friend, who was getting her dog *and* her white oak canopy bed. Housing in Honolulu was very expensive. Kate was never going to have a room big enough for a canopy bed.

There was a lull in the conversation. Her father shifted his feet and then patted the dog's head. "Let's say good-bye to Boggs," he said. "We really have to get going."

He came and rested a hand on Kate's shoulder. She looked up imploringly and then knelt and put her arms around Boggs, her sun-streaked hair falling on his sleek black coat. She breathed in his wonderful dog smell. *I will remember this always*, she thought.

"Come on, Katey girl," her father said softly. "Your brother should be finished loading the car."

How like her sixteen-year-old brother, David, to skip this awful farewell scene with the Lindseys. Kate knew David loved Boggs as much as she did. But there was one important difference. David wanted to move to Honolulu. The airplane this afternoon would be taking him toward his dreams, not away from them.

"Bye, Sara. Bye, Boggs," Kate whispered as the Lindseys led away the unprotesting but doom-struck dog, his tail between his legs. After seeing them out the front door, her father went to check on David's packing.

The mound of suitcases had disappeared from the front hall. All traces of their family had disappeared as well. Before the Lindseys arrived, Kate had double-checked her room. She'd left her backpack on a window seat that was built into a landing halfway up the curved staircase. Now she climbed the stairs to get it, her footsteps echoing in the emptiness.

Upholstered in midnight blue, the window seat looked out on a grove of eucalyptus trees where generations of birds chattered and chirped in a floating canopy of leaves. This was Kate's favorite place in all the world.

The house had been designed by her mother. It had been featured in *Sunset* magazine, with a picture of this window seat and sunshine flickering through the leaves. Kate liked to imagine she used to sit there on her mother's lap, reading *Peter Rabbit* or just listening to the birds and smelling the lemony eucalyptus bark. Her beautiful, silver-blond mother had died nine years before, when Kate was not quite three years old. Having no memories of their time together, she had invented this one.

Kate tried to shut out the going-away sounds from the street below. But it was no use. She could hear Sara coaxing Boggs into their Buick. A car door slammed shut.

"Kate, we really have to leave," her father called up. "There's a lot of traffic on the freeway."

Then came her brother David's baritone voice. "She's probably up in the window seat crying," he said. Kate could visualize the disgusted look on his face.

She wiped the tears on her sleeve and stood up. At the bottom of the stairs, she turned around for one last look, listening to the silence. Then she shrugged into her backpack and went out the front door, closing it gently behind her.

Chapter 2

The flight to Honolulu was full. Every seat in the economy compartment had a passenger squeezed into it. When the man in the next row leaned back, there was no room for Kate to open her meal tray, even if she had wanted to eat. She nudged her father and made a face, pointing at the bald head that was almost resting in her lap.

"It's about time to switch seats," her father said. "When they start serving lunch, you get the window and David gets the aisle. That was the deal you negotiated. Case closed, court adjourned."

"He's not even looking out the window!"

Her brother, David, was reading the latest copy of *Surfing* magazine and pretending not to listen.

"Look, he's making that face again! And you keep poking me with your elbow," Kate said to her father, who was sitting between them trying to read the *L.A.*

Times, which was also intruding into her space.

"And people keep stepping on my feet!"

It was New Year's Day; the airline was serving free champagne. A line of jolly tourists in fluorescent-colored clothes was waiting in the aisle to use the rear lavatories.

"There's plenty of room up in the first-class compartment," Kate said, and got a disapproving look from her father. In the past when she and her brother had gone along on their father's trips, they'd traveled first class. They'd eaten on china plates and sat in armchair seats, with flight attendants bringing drinks whenever they pressed buttons on the control panel.

"Eighteen-inch-wide seats in economy versus twenty-one and a half in first class," David said. "The Kahele Austerity Program strikes again."

That's what David was calling the family's new, no-frills lifestyle. Their house was for sale to help pay for the move to Hawai'i, but California real estate wasn't selling. Meanwhile, their father was going to work for a Hawaiian rights organization called HARA, which had very little money for salaries. The letters stood for something like "Hawaiian Association for Reclaiming Annexed lands," Kate thought, though she wasn't clear on what that meant. He'd be starting work right after the long New Year's weekend. But he wouldn't be paid anything until he passed the Hawai'i State Bar Exam.

Kate's uncle Kimo had said that the government of Hawai'i didn't want any native Hawaiian lawyers coming to fight for their people's stolen land. Uncle insisted that the state would write an even harder exam for someone called Robert Kahele, an easily recognizable Hawaiian name.

Her father just laughed and said that wasn't true, that everyone would take the same exam. You didn't even write your name on your paper, just an assigned number, so the people grading wouldn't know whose they were. All he had to worry about was passing, he said. And that was enough.

Her father was hunched over his newspaper, frowning down at the sports page. Kate could tell he was worried about the exam—and about a lot of other things. Still, *he* was the one who'd made the decision to mess up his life—and Kate's, too.

None of this was my idea, she said to herself. *I was doing just great in California with my friends and my ballet and my house and my dog.*

Her father looked up and shook his head. She wondered if it was something in his Hawaiian blood that made him so good at reading her mind.

"Boggs never would have forgiven us for the four-month quarantine," he said softly.

Hawai'i had a law that pets coming from anywhere else had to spend four months at a government kennel to make sure they weren't carrying rabies. "They could have made an exception," Kate said. "Boggs had all his rabies shots."

"The only exception was for Roy Rogers's horse Trigger," her brother announced, surfacing from behind his magazine. "To entertain the troops during World War Two. Even Seeing Eye dogs have to serve their time in quarantine."

Kate bit her lip. It wasn't worth arguing over the state's quarantine policy, because that wasn't the real reason they'd had to give away their dog. Closing her eyes, could imagine her uncle Kimo saying in his musical waiian accent, *No need ship 'um over heah. Get plenty dogs already.*

Uncle Kimo was a leader in the Hawaiian community, and her father's eldest brother. In Hawaiian families, you really listened to your elders. But Uncle Kimo wasn't very good at listening to anyone else.

Her father was still looking at her with worried eyes.

"Do you hear me complaining?" she said, picking up the airline magazine that was open in her lap. "I'm just sitting here trying to read."

David pulled his gaze away from a full-page photo of a blonde in a yellow bikini. "We could have kept Boggs if we'd moved in with the family," he said. "Uncle Kimo would've let him come."

"Dad, would you make David stop talking to me?"

When her father said nothing, Kate bent her head, determined not to be drawn into the same dumb argument they'd had so many times before. Even if Uncle Kimo had agreed, which she didn't see as very likely, Boggs would have been terrorized by her uncle's scruffy watchdogs. And she would rather sleep on the streets than live in that remote valley on the windward side of the island, a place of mud roads and overarching trees, where there would be daily lectures from Uncle Kimo about her Hawaiian heritage.

David felt differently about the relatives. In the past two summers he'd spent with them, David had become best friends with his cousin Lopaka, Uncle Kimo's son. Uncle Kimo's wife, Auntie Alohi, treated David like one of her own, which meant that she waited on him like he was some kind of royalty. David was completely comfortable with this family that Kate didn't even know how to talk to.

"Let's not reopen that debate," Kate's father said wearily. "The Honolulu apartment was a good choice, at least for this spring semester. It's halfway between the university law library and the HARA offices downtown. And furthermore"—he reached over and tapped David's bikini photo—"I don't want you down at the beach every day. You and I are both going to be hitting the books."

Like their father, David and Kate would be taking a test this spring. Theirs would be a competitive entrance exam to get into Kamehameha, an acclaimed school for children of Hawaiian ancestry and their father's alma mater. Her father was confident Kate would qualify. But David would have to work hard on all subjects, especially math, and he had never been very serious about school.

Kate leaned back, shutting her eyes. No matter how she wiggled around to adjust her neck, she couldn't get comfortable. Her brother's school problems were really the start of this whole disaster, she thought, the reason they were all crammed into economy seats on an airplane flying toward the Hawaiian Islands, which just happened to be the farthest landmass from any other landmass anywhere on Earth.

Two years before, David had been kicked out of his private school for fighting. At the new school, a big public high school, he'd started hanging around with a Pacific Island gang, mostly Hawaiians and Samoans who were clashing with black and Hispanic gangs. Some of them had guns. To get him away from his new buddies, Kate's father had sent David to Uncle Kimo for the summer.

David had responded to Kimo's old-fashioned discipline, to mornings working on the farm and golden afternoons in the surf. He'd returned to Hawai'i for Christmas vacation and then again the following summer. David loved everything about the Islands—the clean air, the sparkling surf, the family picnics with aunties playing ukuleles and a pig roasting in an underground pit.

During her own visit the previous summer, Kate had a hard time even understanding what these relatives were saying. They could speak regular English if they wanted to, but they usually spoke Pidgin, a singsong mixture of English, Hawaiian, Chinese, Japanese, and several other languages. They said "one" instead of "a." They said *wahine* instead of "girl." An all-purpose expression—*da kine*—could mean anything. You had to figure out what the speaker wanted to say. To make things even more confusing, some older relatives spoke Hawaiian, which was yet another language that few people, even Hawaiians, could speak. Sometimes all three languages were mixed up in the same conversation.

But Kate had no trouble understanding the tension in the air whenever they talked about politics. Her uncle's group, the New Hawai'i Nation, wanted to pull out of the United States and become an independent country—and that was only one of the things her uncle and her father disagreed about.

"Visiting family in the Islands?" the flight attendant asked when he reached their row with a tray of free champagne. Her father had already struck up a conversation with the man, who'd recognized her father and brother as fellow "locals." The way her relatives used this word, it meant that a person had dark hair and tan skin and looked Hawaiian, Chinese, Japanese, Filipino, Portuguese, or any combination of the many ethnic groups that made up Hawai'i's mixed population.

Her father sighed. "Moving back home. After twenty years in L.A."

"Hey, *brah*. Major culture shock! You gonna need this!" The man laughed, handing her father a plastic cup of champagne. "But your son there got no worries. Getting set to take on the big waves."

Her brother's magazine was open to a photo of a huge, curling wave about to engulf a tiny surfer who was skimming the surface just ahead of the mountain of water.

"Awesome!" David said, grinning.

"I grew up on the North Shore. Right where they took that picture," the attendant said in his musical accent. "But when the waves get li'dat, I stay watch." He smiled down at Kate, curiosity sparkling in his eyes. "You going surf, too?" he asked.

Kate was used to this kind of question. What he was really asking was, *Are* you *part of this family or what?*

Her father looked like a corporate lawyer in his Armani suit, but once when he'd picked her up at the dance studio wearing shorts, a friend's mother had thought he was her driver. Her father and brother were big-boned and powerful looking, with black hair and bronze skin. They had full lips and high cheekbones, like the South Sea Islanders in travel posters. Anyone could tell they were related, her brother a younger version of their handsome father.

With pale, freckle-dusted skin and blond-streaked hair, Kate didn't look like she belonged to them. At twelve years old, her body was perfect for ballet, thin and delicate. Only the shape of her brown eyes gave any hint of her Polynesian ancestors.

"I don't really like the ocean," she told the flight attendant.

"My daughter," her father said, touching her wrist. He was used to the unspoken questions, too.

The attendant smiled knowingly. "Ah, her mother one *haole?*"

Kate had already noticed how total strangers in

Hawai'i would ask the most personal questions.

Her father nodded. "From Boston. Our daughter got all the Boston genes."

Kate was glad her father had described her inherited genes as "Boston" and not *haole*. She'd visited Hawai'i for just two weeks this past summer. But that word, *haole*, sometimes said as the punch line of a joke and sometimes with a sneer of hatred, was beginning to haunt her.

It meant white people, Caucasians. It meant people who looked like her. From the little Kate knew about Hawai'i's history, there were reasons "locals" might have bad feelings about white people. Still, every time she heard the word, even when it wasn't applied to her, she felt a twinge of fear.

Chapter 3

*H*er aunt and uncle were waiting at the gate, looking uncomfortable in their dress-up clothes. Auntie Alohi's gray-streaked black hair was drawn into a bun with red hibiscus flowers pinned on one side. A red and white *mu'umu'u* flounced down over her plump body. *Mu'umu'u* were the long, loose dresses women in Hawai'i wore. To Kate, it always looked as if they'd forgotten to get dressed and gone outside wearing their nightgowns. They looked even funnier when they had on dressy shoes, like Auntie Alohi's black pumps.

Uncle Kimo wore an orange-flowered *aloha* shirt, the short sleeves stretched tight around his massive arms. Both he and Aunt Alohi carried pink and white flower leis. According to the lei-giving ritual, females presented leis to males and vice versa. Kate knew enough to stand back while Auntie Alohi draped leis around her father's and then her brother's neck.

Her aunt's eyes shone when she bent to kiss David. "*Aloha*," she whispered. "At last you have come home."

Aloha. It meant welcome and homecoming. It meant love.

Then it was Kate's turn. Uncle Kimo towered above her. He carefully arranged the lei around her neck, and she tried not to stiffen when his mustache brushed her cheek. She was never going to get used to all the kissing. Hawaiians kissed with every hello and good-bye. Even complete strangers kissed when they were introduced.

After the greetings they all fell into step behind Uncle Kimo, who walked a head taller than the tourists swirling around him. Without a glance to the right or left, he led them past shops selling plastic leis, hula-dancing dolls, cases of fresh pineapple. And sparkling all around them as they made their way to baggage claim were Hawai'i's colors. Kate had forgotten about the colors, the magenta and orchid leis, the yellow and red flowering bushes, the kelly-green mountains rising above the softer green land. There was a faint smell of flowers in the moist air, which felt soft against her skin.

Her cousin Lopaka was waiting at home. It was quickly arranged that David would go with her uncle and aunt to be reunited with him. The two boys would want to catch a few waves. Kate was grateful when her father, with a quick glance at her, announced that the two of them should settle in at the apartment and start unpacking the boxes that had arrived from California.

Kate didn't want to spend her first night in her

uncle's extra bedroom, with the jungle rustling against the windows. Besides, she was curious about the apartment, wondering what it would be like to go up twelve floors in an elevator to get home.

But they didn't go straight to the apartment after all. They were barely out of the airport parking structure, packed into her uncle's blue station wagon with all the luggage, when her father and uncle got into an argument. It had taken them less than fifteen minutes to find something to debate.

Uncle Kimo was telling her father about a Hawaiian family named Kunia who'd put up a snack stand on Waikīkī Beach without an official government permit. "But state of Hawai'i telling Kunias dey not *allowed* to operate one business on public land. *Public land!*" Uncle Kimo snorted as he eased his battered station wagon onto the freeway. "So dis past Sataday, dey wen' haul away all da stuff. Dey wen' wipe out da stand."

"The Kunias had no right to be there. Waikīkī Beach *is* public land," her father interrupted. "*I'm* almost pure Hawaiian. Can I go claim a piece of Waikīkī and build my house? No! We all have to live by the law."

"Whose law? *We* nevah vote to be part of United States. Dey wen' send in Marines, who wen' aim dere big guns at our palace. Dey lock up our queen. *Annex* our sovereign nation."

Kate knew what the word "sovereign" meant from listening to the arguments this past summer. It meant that Hawaiians used to have their own country, their own government. Uncle Kimo's group, the New Nation, wanted Hawai'i to be a separate country again—with its own language and laws. And Kate could imagine Uncle Kimo as king, wearing the yellow feather cape that was a symbol of royalty.

"We wen' print up leaflets," her uncle was saying. "We stay down Waikīkī. We give 'um to da tourists. Telling dem dey supporting one illegal government! I jus' come from dere." He rummaged in the glove compartment and pulled out a white paper. "Heah, try read dis," he said, handing it to her father.

From the elevated highway, Kate surveyed her new home. On the mountain side, cement apartment buildings and wooden bungalows in pinks, blues, and yellows studded the slopes. To their right, a turquoise sea stretched toward a pale blue horizon. Miles ahead, beyond the curve of Waikīkī hotels, Diamond Head crater nosed its way into the Pacific.

"Where's our apartment?" Kate asked, leaning forward.

Her father didn't hear the question. Auntie Alohi, who was squeezed between Kate and David in the back seat, pointed toward the mountains. "Over there. *Mauka* side of the freeway."

Kate couldn't remember what *mauka* meant, but she didn't ask. In her previous visit there had been so many unfamiliar words that she'd stopped trying to understand what people were saying.

David was gazing at the ocean, showing no interest in

the apartment. "Did Lopaka get his new board?" he asked.

Auntie Alohi nodded, the large hibiscus flowers wobbling on her head. "For Christmas. Cousin Kalani using the old board now." After a moment she said, "Auntie Ruth *hāpai*. Baby due in July."

"Cool!" David said, and nodded toward Kate, a superior smile on his face. "My sister doesn't understand Pidgin. *Hāpai* means 'pregnant.'"

"No worry." Alohi reached out shyly to pat Kate's hand. "We help her." And turning to David, she said, "*Hāpai* is one Hawaiian word. Get plenty Hawaiian words in Pidgin."

Kate turned away and pretended to look at the green mountains. It was all too strange. The language, the glaring sunshine, the swarm of relatives. Everyone was related in some way to everyone else. Kate would never be able to keep track of who they all were. She couldn't even remember which one was Auntie Ruth, who was *hāpai*.

In the front seat her father was gesturing with the white paper. "I can't believe you're doing this," he was saying. "Tourists provide millions of dollars in revenue a year. Everyone depends on them, including Hawaiians."

It was amazing how much these two brothers found to argue about. Why couldn't they joke about their golf games, like her friends' fathers in California?

Kate wondered if her aunt was as sick of listening to them as she was. Alohi's cinnamon-brown face showed no emotion. Her fleshy hands were folded in her lap, and she looked straight ahead. Did she agree with Uncle Kimo about complete independence? Did she have any opinions of her own? She seemed to exist only to wait on people and cook food. Underneath that silence, you never knew what she was thinking.

Kate closed her eyes and tried to imagine what Boggs was doing back in California. Part of her wanted him to be happy in his new home. The other part wished he would refuse to eat, or bite the mailman, so that the Lindseys would have to send him back.

"You're giving the sovereignty cause a bad name," her father was yelling. "These tourists will think we're all a bunch of nuts!"

"Not!" Uncle shouted.

Kate fell against her aunt's solid bulk as Uncle veered into an exit lane marked WAIKĪKĪ.

"*I show you!*" Uncle said. "We give pepas to tourists and dey stay reading 'um. Some even asking questions. I show you!"

Kate frowned over at her brother. She knew he wanted to get to the windward side of the island, to his cousin, to the endless rolling waves. But even David didn't argue. Maybe he was afraid of Uncle Kimo sometimes, too.

"We all go beach tomorrow," Uncle Kimo announced. "Not Waikīkī, though. *'A'ole!* We go other side. Where dey nevah spoil 'um with dis concrete jungle. Eh, Kaleo," he said to David. "You can try Lopaka's new board."

Her uncle and aunt always called David by his Hawaiian middle name, Kaleo, and her father by his Hawaiian name, Ikaika. Kate had a Hawaiian middle name, too—Maluhia—but they didn't call her by any name.

Within minutes, they were off the freeway and negotiating traffic in Waikīkī's wide avenues.

Uncle parked in a no parking zone. He didn't believe in obeying traffic laws or paying parking tickets, because his group had already voted to drop out of the United States. The yellow license plate on Uncle's old blue station wagon said just one word, SOVEREIGN, in bold red letters.

"Do a lot of Hawaiians have those plates?" Kate asked as they were walking to the beach.

"No more Hawaiians!" Uncle exploded. "Just like your dad, you keep on using *haole* name for our people. I wen' tell you last summer, we *kanaka maoli!"*

Her father rubbed his forehead with his index and middle fingers. "It means, 'the real people,'" he said to Kate. "But the term 'Hawaiian' is also acceptable."

Kate followed behind them on the sidewalk. Now it wasn't even safe to use the word "Hawaiian"! How was she supposed to remember the other, *kanaka* something, from last summer, her first visit to Hawai'i since she was a baby?

They didn't see any New Nation members passing out leaflets until after they'd gone into one of the hotels. Uncle Kimo led them to a table in a beachside café. He ordered beers for the adults and sodas for Kate and David without asking what kind they wanted.

Uncle pointed. "Dat's where they wen' destroy Kunias' rental stand. See da Hawaiian flag? We hang 'um upside down. Symbolizes sovereignty movement."

"An upside-down flag is an international sign of distress," her father explained. "The Hawaiian people are in distress, but sending tourists home is not the answer." He was drumming his fingers on the tabletop, the way he always did when he was trying to have patience and not yell at her brother.

Uncle dismissed him with a dark look. "See dat *wahine* in the blue *mu'umu'u?*" he said.

Beyond the restaurant's low cement wall, the woman and two men were passing out the white papers. The woman had just handed a leaflet to a blonde sprawled on a beach blanket. Clutching the strings of her bikini top, the girl squinted at the white paper, shaking her head.

Farther down on the beach, the two men gave leaflets to a man in white pants and a woman in a green dress.

"Tourists living like kings ovah hea," Uncle Kimo said, with a sweep of his arm, "while our bruddahs and sistahs living on da beach with no roof over dere heads!" He pointed with his chin at the adjacent hotel, which was painted pink with green-trimmed turrets and curved balconies.

"Disneyland," Uncle said, looking sternly at Kate and David. "Dey wen' take our precious *'aina* and make one Disneyland."

'Aina. That was one word Kate knew because her uncle used it all the time. It meant "land." But land meant something different in Hawai'i than it did in California. People here said the word with a kind of worship in their voices.

Still arguing about the tourist industry, her father and uncle went to talk to the New Nation woman in the blue *mu'umu'u.* David wandered over to check out the hotel's rental surfboards. Auntie Alohi sat quietly, hands folded in her lap.

Kate didn't want to be left alone with her aunt. All her friends' mothers back in California talked a lot, especially Mrs. Lindsey. Their housekeeper, Mrs. Gomez, had always chatted as she worked, asking Kate about school and telling stories in her Spanish-accented English. Mrs. Gomez had lived a tough childhood, but she could still look back at things that happened and find something to laugh about. Kate suspected there was some kind of survival lesson in those stories, because Mrs. Gomez always came up with one after Kate had had a bad day at school or had been scolded by her ballet teacher.

So her aunt's silence made Kate nervous. After all, the adult was supposed to start the conversation and keep it going. *I'm just a kid,* Kate thought. *What am I supposed to say to someone who just sits there looking out at the ocean?* Kate bent to roll up her jeans. "I'm gonna go get my feet wet," she said. Her aunt just smiled and nodded.

The water was deliciously cool, the sand soft as cloth

under her bare feet. A sailboat shimmered on the horizon; an airplane glinted overhead. Hula music was drifting from the pink hotel. Kate liked the ukulele rhythm, the soft vowels of the Hawaiian singer. She liked the pink hotel with its gingerbread trim. She took a deep breath of salty air. The water was a translucent blue, and everything around was clean and sparkling and new. No wonder Uncle Kimo didn't like it. Not enough mud. Kate decided that Waikīkī was the only part of Hawai'i she *did* like.

Something grazed her arm, and she turned around, expecting to see her brother.

But it was one of the men from the New Nation. Without a word, he pressed a white paper into her hand.

GO HOME! the leaflet announced in large black letters. YOU ARE SUPPORTING AN ILLEGAL GOVERNMENT BY YOUR PRESENCE HERE IN THESE ISLANDS. IN 1893, THE UNITED STATES MARINES ILLEGALLY MARCHED ON THE SOVEREIGN NATION OF HAWAI'I. . . .

"I *want* to go home! *So there!*" she screamed at their retreating backs. "You can keep your precious *'aina!*"

Clutching the paper in her fist, she turned and ran back to the hotel.

Chapter 4

"*I* want to explain about the leaflet," Kate's father said later that night at the apartment.

Kate was in her new bedroom, surrounded by cardboard boxes, their contents spilling onto the ten-by-ten-foot floor space. She shrugged and waved him into the room, which contained a fake-wood dresser and a single bed her aunt had covered with a quilt in a green pineapple pattern. Auntie said the quilt had been made by Kate's grandmother, who had died before she was born.

Her father had to move a pile of ballet clothes to sit down on the bed. "Why don't you leave this for tomorrow," he said. "It's after ten. That's after midnight California time."

Kate had been trying to find the box that contained her pale blue comforter from California. She didn't want to tell her father that she didn't like his dead mother's quilt, that it was too gaudy.

"I can't sleep, so I might as well unpack." She got up from the floor and went over to the window. It felt strange being alone in the apartment with him. Back in California, Kate was usually alone with the housekeeper in the evening, while David was out cruising with friends and her father was working. She liked to do homework at the kitchen table while Mrs. Gomez bustled around packing lunches and cleaning up. Her father wouldn't come home until late. He would eat dinner in the breakfast nook with some legal brief spread out next to his plate. If Kate was still at the kitchen table, he would joke that they both had homework to do. Then Mrs. Gomez would say something like, "Not this señorita. She's going off to her beautiful bed, fit for a princess," and to Kate, with a hug, "Go give your papa a good-night kiss. Make his day."

The great lawyer, never at a loss for words, looked ill at ease now, sitting on her cluttered bed, like he didn't know what to say. Kate knew her father loved her. He had a way of smiling at her with his eyes, and he almost always had made time to attend her ballet performances, even if he had to come late. One of his reasons for this move to Hawai'i had been to have more time to spend with his children. But he didn't have much practice in talking to her, or to David either, for that matter.

"You don't have to explain anything," she said. "They know I don't belong here, Uncle's friends."

Her father picked up a pink toe shoe and stroked the smooth satin. After a moment he said, "Do you remember when David was expelled from Saint Steven's?"

"For hitting that kid who called him nigger. Peter something."

"Peter Salvio. He'd been calling David nigger since first grade. One day, seven years later, David had enough."

"What's that got to do with the leaflet?"

"People react differently to racial cruelty. Some hit back. Others find it difficult to trust anyone who looks like their persecutors. . . ." He sat looking down at the pineapple pattern on the quilt before continuing. "And some of us decide to escape."

"Escape from what?"

"From ourselves," her father said softly. "Some people called *us* niggers when we were growing up here. Stupid Hawaiians." He rubbed his forehead with his index and middle fingers. "It was worse for Uncle. Kimo's darker than me. He was always out working in the taro patch while I was inside with my face in some book. Skin color made a big difference back then; you didn't want to look Hawaiian. Everybody wanted to be white. . . ."

Kate turned to face him, leaning against the cool windowpane.

"I thought if I worked hard enough, I could build a life where no one would dare call me nigger."

Kate wanted to ask if that was why he had married her mother, who was blond and blue eyed, as *haole* as it is possible to be.

"When I was in law school, I was too busy studying

to come home," he said. "Then I was too busy making my way in the firm. It's a Hawaiian custom to bring your baby home for a special *luʻau* on the first birthday. But when your brother was one year old, I was too busy to make the trip. Uncle Kimo called me a coconut. Brown on the outside, white on the inside." He laughed. "We got into a big fight over the phone."

He got up and joined Kate at the window. "I know this move isn't easy for you. All you've given up." He handed her the toe shoe. "We'll find you a ballet school as soon as we get settled."

"We won't have the money, not until the house sells."

"We'll find money for that."

"What did Uncle Kimo—your family—think of my mother?"

"They only met her twice. At our wedding in California, and then once in Hawaiʻi. When she talked me into bringing *you* back for your first birthday *luʻau*."

"Were they mad at you for marrying her?"

"They didn't know what to make of her. Don't look at me like that—*her* family, what was left of them, never even *came* to our wedding! The Boston relatives wanted nothing to do with us. Your mother betrayed them by marrying a colored."

Her father was talking like a lawyer, doing what he himself called "skirting the issue." But Kate knew what Uncle Kimo must have thought of his *haole* sister-in-law from Boston.

"I was glad to have nothing to do with her family," he said. "But your mother was fascinated with mine. She read up on Hawai'i's history, on the hula and chants. 'It's a dying culture,' I kept telling her. 'Let it rest in peace.' *She's* the one who insisted you and your brother have Hawaiian middle names. And not just translations of English names that the missionaries introduced. Real Hawaiian names."

Nodding at Kate's expression of surprise, he said, "Your mother researched the old customs. Children used to be named for personal characteristics they would bring to their families. Kaleo Nui, your brother's full name, means 'the big voice.'"

"That suits him. Mr. Know-It-All. Always talking."

"Your mother was right about the names. About preserving the language." He shook his head. "And I'd worked so hard to leave all that behind. My language. My name. . . . After your mother died, I worked even harder, making partner, joining the country club, playing golf. You had to play golf."

They stood looking out the window. Beyond the ribbon of freeway marched a jagged line of skyscrapers, their windows glistening in the blue velvet sky.

"Our parents were punished for speaking Hawaiian," he said. "Even on the school playground. We grew up ashamed of who we were."

"What happened to make you change your mind— about living here and all?"

"When I brought David back here two years ago,

things were different. Hawaiians were different. We used to accept the status quo. No more! There were public schools where children were reading and writing and learning math *in Hawaiian*. With waiting lists to get into them!" He was silent a moment, staring into the fragrant tropic night. "At first there were just some legal issues I wanted to research. After I got back to California, I started talking to other Native Americans."

"You went to that Indian reservation."

"The Lakota Nation," he corrected. "The Lakota won a court case against the United States government. Nobody thought they could win, but they did! They had good lawyers! They won the right to run their own schools, preserve their language, manage their streams and lands. An Indian nation inside the state of Montana! It gave me hope for Hawai'i. That's the model of sovereignty HARA is pushing for." His lips tightened. "I just wish we could get Uncle to buy into it. He still wants the whole state."

Off to their left, the great mass of Diamond Head crater was silhouetted, a shade darker than the sky. Shadowy mountains, like guardians of older times, loomed above valleys studded with electric lights.

"Uncle's right about one thing, though. We Hawaiians cannot abandon our land. Our people have been here to cherish and protect it for more than two thousand years. I had an obligation to bring back my skills—my knowledge of the law—and put them to work here."

"What does my middle name mean?" Kate asked.

"Maluhia means 'peace,' but there's more to your name than just that. What's actually written on your birth certificate is 'Kama Hoʻomaluhia i ka Laʻi.' I think the translation is more like 'peacemaker.' We can ask Uncle, or better yet, Auntie. She grew up speaking Hawaiian." He smiled sadly. "I'm the one who got into Kamehameha, the special school for children of Hawaiian ancestry. But you couldn't study Hawaiian. Only French and Spanish. It's changed now. Hawaiian is the most popular language taught. I hope you and David will get to study it, too." He put his arm around her. "That's why we came back. I wanted us to be part of the change. And part of this land."

With Uncle Kimo, even a trip to the beach had to begin with a sermon. He pointed toward a collection of tents and lean-tos at the curve of the bay. "Our people, *kanaka maoli*. Taking back our stolen beaches. But government telling 'um get out." Kate followed her father and uncle toward the dozen or so Hawaiians gathered at the tents, while David and their cousin Lopaka raced for the water with their surfboards. Kate had worn a bathing suit underneath her shorts, but one look at the crashing waves convinced her to stay onshore. She was afraid of the same surf that lured her brother to its bone-crushing breakers.

Kate found a patch of shade under a tarpaulin and sat hugging her knees while her father and uncle talked with the beach protesters. After a while two girls came out of the nearest tent and stood staring at her. With her pale hair and white skin, she must have looked just as strange to them as she felt. She could barely understand the adult conversation. Even her father had shifted into Pidgin. She wondered how he could still speak it after so many years away.

At least he didn't seem as angry as he had the day before with Uncle Kimo at Waikīkī. Kate watched him talking to a chocolate-brown, gray-bearded Hawaiian who seemed to be the leader. Uncle Kimo was listening, too, and not making speeches.

Auntie Alohi had stayed home to organize the welcome *luʻau*. At dawn the uncles had wrapped a pig in banana leaves and buried it in the underground oven, an *imu*. Kate knew the routine from the previous summer. Later that afternoon they would dig it out of the ashes, and the aunties would carry baskets of *poi* and salmon to the big tables on Uncle's covered *lānai*. Kate was praying they wouldn't all get indigestion from listening to the two brothers argue during the meal.

The older of the two girls stood framed in the tent opening. Her face sullen, she was twisting a lock of black hair around her index finger. "You like beef?" she asked, catching Kate's eye.

Kate shook her head, squinting in the sun's glare. She didn't understand the words, but she knew there was nothing friendly about the question. Her heart started to race. Without looking at the girl, Kate got up and went to stand next to her father.

"What does 'beef' mean in Pidgin?" Kate asked her brother when they were back in the car.

"Beef?" David turned to her, his hair dark and sleek with water, his eyelashes glistening. He looked like a beautiful sea creature from a world she could never hope to share.

"Who wen' tell you dat?" Lopaka wanted to know.

"A girl from the tents. She asked me if I like beef."

"You like *beef!*" Lopaka mimicked, shaking with laughter, and her brother said, "Beef means 'fight.' She was asking you to fight."

"Watch out. Dat girl one *tita*," Lopaka said, still laughing.

"She doesn't even know me. Why would she want to fight?" But Kate knew the answer. *Because I look like a* haole. *Even if I'm trailing along behind some Hawaiians, I don't belong in this place.*

"*Titas*, dey always like fight," Lopaka said. "Don't need no reason."

The hot wind blowing in the car windows made a tangle of Kate's fine hair, which was plastered to her neck. She missed the air-conditioned cars back home in California. She missed everything about California so much, she didn't dare think about it or she would start to cry.

"*Tita* is Pidgin for a tough girl," David said. Then,

after a silence, he added, "Just don't ever let them know you're scared. You're gonna have to hang tough when you get to school on Monday. It won't be anything like Saint Theresa's."

Chapter 5

"Kathryn Maluhia Kahele . . ." Mrs. Odo, Kate's new teacher, read her name from the orange registration card. "We're very happy to have you join our class," she said, smiling.

Kate smiled back. Mrs. Odo, a middle-aged Japanese American, looked trim and attractive in a blue linen dress and matching shoes. Even Mrs. Lindsey, Sara's elegant mother, would have approved of the outfit. Kate felt some of the tension drain from between her shoulders. Her teacher seemed genuinely happy to have a new student; she had a lovely smile that wrinkled the corners of her eyes.

"First things first," Mrs. Odo was saying. "The bell is about to ring, and the thundering herds will be upon us. We'll need to find you a desk. Mehana!"—Mrs. Odo beckoned to a girl who was working at a computer in the back of the classroom—"Would you come help our new student get settled? There's that empty desk in your pod."

The girl got up and came toward them, smiling shyly. She was slim and graceful with long brown hair that swayed as she walked.

"She'll need a math book and one of the novels for literature study," Mrs. Odo said. "Maybe you can help her choose one. Oh, there it goes!"

A bell buzzed, and students erupted into the room.

There were no neat rows facing the teacher. Instead, the classroom was arranged in four pods, or clusters, of six desks, all facing one another. Mehana showed Kate to an empty seat at her pod and went off to find a math book.

Kate sat there wearing a fixed smile, unable to find anything to say to a couple of boys who were studying her with unmasked curiosity. She concentrated on not letting fear show on her face. Saint Theresa's was an all-girls school, and there were only a few boys in her ballet troupe. She'd never been in a room with so many boys, boys of all sizes and shades. Small, wiry, Asian-looking boys and six-foot Hawaiians or Samoans—Kate couldn't tell them apart—who towered over Mrs. Odo. The boys were noisier than the girls and in almost constant motion, swinging at one another, knocking books off the desks.

Two of the noisiest were seated at the next pod. One was tall and fat and reminded Kate of a statue of the Buddha she'd seen in a museum. Kids were calling him

Richard. His companion was short and skinny with shoulder-length reddish-brown hair that hung over his eyes in straight bangs.

By the time Mrs. Odo got them all seated, Mehana was back, showing Kate where they were in the math book. "Decimals, ugh," she said, pointing to the chapter review.

Kate could only smile her frozen smile and nod. She'd finished with decimals two years before in her advanced math class back home. All she could think about was that her clothes were all wrong. No one else was wearing a funky hat or a plaid shirt with overall shorts. The black felt hat with the floppy brim was her favorite. She'd always wanted to be allowed to wear it to school. The long-sleeved shirt had been comfortable in the cool morning air when Kate first got up. But it had been a stupid choice for a hot, un-air-conditioned class-room. She really had no idea how kids dressed to go to school. At Saint Theresa's everyone wore the same middy blouse, navy skirt, and gray blazer.

All the girls in this classroom had long, dark hair. Kate pulled her hat over her blond-streaked hair. She'd had it cut in a short pageboy just before leaving California, on Mrs. Lindsey's advice.

She wondered if her father was still in the parking lot. She had insisted on facing the new classroom alone. Now she wanted to run after him and beg him to take her back to California.

"I'd like to introduce a new student," Mrs. Odo

announced to the class. "This is Kathryn Maluhia Kahele."

Kate's heart was pounding so loudly, she was sure everyone in the pod could hear it. She was having trouble catching her breath.

"Do you want to go by your Hawaiian or your English name?" Mrs. Odo was asking.

"She not Hawaiian! She one *haole!*" The shout came from the skinny boy with the reddish hair.

"Shut up, Chad!" Mehana hissed at him. "She's probably *hapa*."

Hapa? Kate frantically searched her memory. *Hapa?* Where had she had heard that word before? What was Mehana saying about her? *Something was wrong.* "Wait . . . no!" she said aloud, gulping for air. "I'm *not* pregnant!"

Her announcement produced chaos. Chad doubled over laughing and then fell on the floor. Richard, his fat friend, started thumping on the desk, chanting. "She pregnant, she *hāpai!*"

Mrs. Odo silenced them with a stern face. "It is rude to laugh at a newcomer, and also very cruel. Kathryn, *hapa* means 'part' in Pidgin and in Hawaiian. Mehana was saying that many people here are part Hawaiian and part Caucasian. They're called *hapa haole*."

"*Hāpai* means pregnant," Mehana whispered.

Mrs. Odo must have heard her. "It's a natural error," she said with a fierce look at Chad, who was laughing again.

Kate studied her hands. They looked very white on

the brown desktop, the freckles stark against her pale skin. She felt her face burning. She wanted to disappear, to wake up from this bad dream and be back in her canopy bed. She wanted to jump on the next plane to California and show up on Mrs. Gomez's doorstep. The housekeeper would have to take her in. *How could my father do this to me?* she cried to herself. *He couldn't do this if he loved me.*

At lunch Chad followed her around, calling, "Stupid *haole.*" Richard came up behind her and chanted, "She pregnant. She *hāpai,*" when she was scraping her untouched fish sticks into the garbage. Kate could hear the giggles as she left the cafeteria.

The rest of the day passed in a blur. Walking home, she couldn't remember a single thing she had done, a single word she'd written in her notebook.

By the time she reached the apartment, a ten-minute walk, she was choking back tears of rage. Why hadn't her father prepared her? Why hadn't David explained what it would be like, instead of vague warnings about needing to "hang tough"?

She didn't want to see either one of them. She took the elevator to the twelfth floor, determined to get to her room before she started crying. She was praying her father would be out picking up her brother at his new high school.

Both were at the apartment, waiting for her. And to make the most miserable day of her life one notch more miserable, Uncle Kimo was there, too. Her father and uncle were sitting in the living room. She slipped past them into the kitchen, where David was at the counter, cutting up carrots.

"Here," he said, handing Kate a paring knife and some stalks of celery. "Uncle is teaching us how to make stew, Hawaiian style. Make yourself useful."

Kate picked up the knife, afraid of the rush of anger, afraid of how much she wanted to hurt her brother. Her hands were shaking.

"That bad, huh?"

"*How else could it be? I'm a* haole!" She threw the knife onto the cutting board. "*Hang tough!*" she yelled. "What kind of stupid advice is that?"

"You have to give it right back to them. It'll be worse if you let them push you around. . . ."

"Well, that's something you'll never have to worry about—with your nice brown skin," she sobbed. "Did your friends tell you about Kill-*Haole* Day? It happens every spring, the last day of school. All you locals will have a great time."

She raced to her room, slamming the door behind her. When she heard her father coming down the hall, she twisted the lock.

"Kate. Come out and talk to us," her father said softly.

"How could you do this to me? You knew what it would be like!"

"It's just one semester at Waiala School," her father said. "Things'll be better next fall at Kamehameha."

"Why would Kamehameha be any better for someone who looks like me?"

"She's had a totally protected life," she heard her brother say. "She's gotta learn to fight back if she's gonna survive here. In any school."

There was a short silence, and then Uncle Kimo said, "She jus' gotta get more tough."

Chapter 6

*K*ate's father didn't agree about the toughening up. He insisted that every child—no matter how different—had the right to go to school without being harassed. He got into an argument with Uncle Kimo right there in the hallway outside her door.

"*Are you satisfied?*" She heard her father's voice getting shrill. "Because people like you are fueling this anti-*haole* sentiment!"

Kate held a pillow over her head, her tears making a wet spot on her old comforter. She'd found it in one of the boxes from California and packed away her grandmother's pineapple quilt. But the pale blue didn't go with the brown carpeting and the fake-wood dresser, where her aunt had arranged some gardenias in a vase. Nothing helped. The room was depressingly ugly.

After a while, the three of them moved back to the living room. They went on talking—mostly Uncle Kimo was talking. Kate could hear the murmur of voices, but not the words. As the sky deepened to blue-violet, she began to get thirsty. She wanted to call Mrs. Gomez and ask her for a good survival story, but the telephone was in the living room. She heard the doorbell ring, and soon afterward, the smell of pizza drifted down the hallway. Kate hadn't eaten anything since breakfast. Still, she was surprised she could feel hunger at a time like this, when her life was ruined.

She didn't leave her room until she heard her uncle leave for home. Her father was at the table in the dining area with law books spread out around him. He jumped up when he saw her, a pained look in his eyes.

"I'm hungry," Kate said.

He came and hugged her. "Katey girl," he said. They stood a moment listening to the rumble of cars on the freeway two blocks away. "We can talk about it whenever you're ready," he said. "First, we get you some food. We called out for pizza. David made his first salad. It was very . . . creative."

"Hawaiian stew is rescheduled for tomorrow night," David yelled from the bedroom.

Kate sat down at the table and took a bite of pizza. Haltingly, she began to tell her father about Mrs. Odo and Mehana, and finally about Chad and Richard.

Her father's mouth was tight, and he was drumming his fingers on the table. "I'll go with you tomorrow. Get you switched to another class."

"You can't do that. . . ." David came bounding from

the bedroom. "Those guys are just talking stink," he said, reaching for the last slice of pizza. "You have to give it right back to them."

"Children have the right to be protected from verbal abuse—"

"Don't argue, please," Kate interrupted. "Changing classes isn't going to help. They don't bother me during class. The problem is at lunchtime. Tomorrow I'll ask if I can eat in the classroom."

David gave a snort of frustration. "You don't get it. They just want to find out if you can take it."

"No, *you* don't get it!" Her father's voice was getting louder. "Richard and Chad are perpetuating the same racism that used to be inflicted on Hawaiian children. On Uncle and me when we were in school. Stupid Hawaiian, stupid *haole*. It's a vicious cycle—"

"You turned out okay!" David shot back.

The pizza was a lump in Kate's throat. "Dad, listen," she said. "There *is* something you can do for me at school. You can ask them to take my Hawaiian name off my record. I don't want anyone to call me Maluhia." She saw her father's disappointment and explained, "I don't want to have to prove I'm Hawaiian because I don't look like one. They'll just make fun of me and call me *hapa*."

David was getting ready to protest.

"I'm not going to . . . talk stink back to them," she said to him, and then, softly, "I can't do that."

"You're gonna have to face up to this," David said. "It won't go away!"

"You don't know what it's like!" Her heart was thumping in her ears.

"What do you think I had to put up with *every day of my life* in California?" David shouted as she ran out of the room.

The next morning Kate asked Mrs. Odo if she could eat lunch in the room. For a moment, her teacher looked at her with a sad smile, as if she wanted to say something and couldn't find the right words. Then she patted Kate's arm. "Sure you can. And you can stay in during recess to straighten up the classroom library if you'd like. That would be a big help." Kate was grateful. Mrs. Odo hadn't told her she needed to hang tough.

She thought she would not be able to survive one more day at Waiala Elementary. But she got through a second day, then a third, and then a fourth. Richard made faces whenever Kate looked his way. She learned to keep her eyes downcast. Chad whispered, "Stupid *haole*" whenever students were moving around the classroom and Mrs. Odo wasn't looking. Kate learned to tune him out, to pretend she was someplace else, like back home dancing ballet or else throwing a Frisbee for Boggs under the eucalyptus trees. The other students left her alone, as if she'd grown invisible.

And she wanted to stay invisible. A couple of bigger girls strutted around the school giving people bad looks, which were called "stink eye." Kate guessed they were *titas* and stayed clear. They left her alone. Most frightening

were Richard and Chad. Even though Chad was small
for his age, she heard Mehana say that he was in trouble
with the police for beating up a young tourist down in
Waikīkī. Where could it come from, she wondered, the
kind of rage that would make you want to harm someone
you didn't even know?

Kate couldn't figure out why certain kids got pushed
around and others didn't. One thing was clear, though. It
wasn't any good being a *haole* in public school. According
to her brother, it was even worse at the high school, and
he kept up his warnings about the need to act tough. One
night David told her about a newcomer from California
who'd been suspended by his feet over a fourth-floor bal-
cony by a gang of boys. None of the teachers had been
around. "There's not always going be someone there to
protect *you*, either," he added.

"You want to sign me up for karate class?"

"That wouldn't be such a bad idea. I keep telling you,
you can't let them get you on the run in the first place!"

"I'm handling it, okay?"

"Yeah, sure. You hide in the classroom at lunch."

She turned on the TV and blasted the volume to cut
off his advice.

Another week began. She survived each new day by
staying close to Mrs. Odo. She carried her isolation like
a weight in her heart. Often the kids in her pod seemed
to be speaking a foreign language, words like *lolo* and
akamai and *pau*, which she'd heard her relatives say, too.
Even the schoolwork was strange, compared to Saint

Theresa's. Instead of studying textbooks and filling out worksheets, students read real novels in small groups called "literature circles." They were supposed to talk about the stories, about similar feelings and experiences they'd had. In math they were *supposed* to help one another work out the problems.

A big Hawaiian girl named Rebecca sat next to Chad. Kate wasn't sure if Rebecca was a *tita*, but she acted very tough with him. Every math period she had to nag him to open his book and then she had to get up and find him a pencil, which he never seemed to have. Meanwhile, Chad tried to make her laugh, or he threw paper airplanes at Richard. Amazingly, Rebecca was usually able to get him to settle down and do some of the problems.

Mrs. Odo soon figured out that Kate already knew everything in the math book. She took her aside and asked if she could sit next to a new girl named Jung Hee and help her catch up. Jung Hee, who had just arrived from Korea, needed much more attention than Mrs. Odo could give her. Kate didn't mind working with Jung Hee, who was an outsider like herself and who seemed just as scared. Kate was actually grateful for something to do; it helped her get through the day.

On Friday after lunch Mrs. Odo told them about a schoolwide talent show coming up in March. Their class would be contributing a dance number. "Mehana has volunteered to teach us a hula," the teacher said, glancing over at their pod.

Mehana was the most beautiful girl Kate had ever

seen. Her honey-colored skin was a shade lighter than her long, silky hair. Her almond eyes held flecks of gold, and she moved with an effortless grace. *I should have known she was a dancer,* Kate thought to herself as she watched Mehana walk to the front of the classroom.

Mrs. Odo turned on the music, and Mehana seemed to float across the floor, her hips and long hair swaying to the ukulele rhythm. The words of the song were in Hawaiian, but her beautiful hands told of the moon and stars, of fragrant flowers and fluttering palm trees.

Kate had thought hula was something for tourists, girls in plastic skirts dancing to silly songs about tiny bubbles in the champagne. Mehana's hula was different—a way of telling stories without words, a kind of body poetry. In its own way it was every bit as polished as ballet. And Kate knew from experience that Mehana's effortless grace must have taken years of hard work to achieve.

Watching Mehana's fingertips reaching out for the softness of the air, Kate felt a bubbling of excitement, a spurt of joy she hadn't felt since the last time she herself had danced. She struggled to remember when that was. Before Christmas vacation, they'd danced in the chorus from *Swan Lake* at the L.A. Museum Theater. The ballet troupe gave her a going-away party afterward. It seemed so far away, years instead of weeks.

The song ended, and the class applauded. Even Chad and Richard had no put-downs to deliver.

Mrs. Odo said, "Students who want to be in the performance can give us your names. We especially need some courageous boys."

There was laughter as Richard pointed to Chad. "Chad like try," he said, doing a mock hula with his hands. Ignoring him, Rebecca and five other girls raised their hands to volunteer.

When Mehana came back to their pod, Kate said, "You're a wonderful dancer."

"Thanks! Would you like to learn? We'll be practicing lunchtime and after school."

"Can not!" Chad yelled out. "She not Hawaiian!"

"Shut up, Chad," Mehana said, "you don't have to be Hawaiian to dance hula." She turned back to Kate. "Don't listen to him."

But Kate had lowered her head over her book. "Thanks, anyway," she murmured. "I have to go right home after school."

After dismissal Chad crept up behind her chair. "You walk home all alone, *hāpai* girl?" he said into her ear.

Heart thudding, she spun around to face him. He stood a moment, grinning his threat, then turned and ran off.

Chapter 7

*K*ate was sorry to hear that life in California was going on just fine without her. She got a card with a ballerina on it from Mrs. Gomez, who was working for a Chinese couple with twin boys. They were a nice family, the housekeeper wrote, but she missed her favorite ballerina very much. Sara Lindsey called to say Boggs was swimming in the lake and catching a Frisbee. On Saturday Mrs. Lindsey was taking Sara and a friend to a Bolshoi Ballet performance and then to Kate's favorite Mexican restaurant.

That same Saturday morning Kate woke up from a dream about Saturdays back in California; this was her favorite day of the week. After a two-hour ballet class, she usually went for lunch and shopping with Sara and her mother. But she didn't want to remember buying avocado face masks with Sara at the mall. She didn't want to think about cool, misty mornings with Mrs. Gomez making pancakes and singing in Spanish. She got out of bed and went into the tiny kitchen, where she shook some cold cereal into a bowl. In Honolulu, Hawai'i, the morning was sunny and hot.

"You're supposed to be getting dressed in throwaway clothes," David yelled from the bedroom he shared with their father.

Kate took her cereal over to the dinette table, where her father was studying. She sat looking out at the Waikīkī skyline through the sliding doors to the tiny *lānai*. When she didn't answer, David came out to the living room. "Come on, *'awīwī*," he said. "Uncle's on his way to pick us up."

"I don't have any throwaway clothes," she said, imagining Sara at the Bolshoi Ballet in her Laura Ashley dress. "And I don't want to go to Uncle's farm."

Her father looked up from his books. "I'll be studying here all day. I don't want you stuck in the apartment."

"I think I have a fever."

"Let's see." He pushed aside a stack of papers and reached for her forehead. "Feels okay to me. David, make sure she puts on plenty of sunblock. She's still so pale."

"I'm too pale to be pulling weeds in a taro field. Can't I just hang around and read?"

"You don't pull weeds," David interrupted, "you mash them down into the mud with your feet." He flashed his most superior grin. "Definitely not your thing. And it's not a taro field. It's called a *lo'i*."

"Just stay inside with Auntie until it's time to go to the beach," her father said.

Rummaging in a drawer, Kate found an old pair of shorts and a faded blue T-shirt. There was one thing worse than being barefoot in the mud, and that was hanging around the house with her silent aunt, trying to figure out what she was thinking. Kate jammed a towel and bathing suit into her backpack. How like Uncle to demand that she and her brother and assorted cousins earn their beach picnic by working in his mud patch all morning!

During her visit the past summer, Kate had avoided this Saturday morning ritual, but she hadn't managed to avoid the lectures on taro, which Uncle called *kalo*, using the old Polynesian pronunciation. He liked to remind them that even King Kamehameha the Great had worked in the royal taro patch every morning.

Uncle never let anyone forget that the Kaheles were one of the few families still raising their own taro in the traditional way. Whenever the *lo'i* needed clearing, Uncle would gather as many family members as he could and march them up to the terraces behind his house.

Later that morning Kate stood on a grassy walk looking down on these same family terraces. Some of the rectangular *lo'i* were planted with jade-green taro, the heart-shaped leaves swaying in the breeze. Others were empty and flooded with water. The one Uncle had led them to was full of weeds, which some cousins, aunts, and uncles were stomping down into the mud.

Only Kate remained outside the *lo'i*, trying to tuck her fine hair into a ponytail clip. The sides weren't long enough and kept falling out.

Uncle Kimo was in up to his knees; mud was smeared on his muscular arms and white T-shirt, which was transparent with perspiration. He had already cleared a large section with his big, wide feet. But he still had enough energy to order people around.

"You boys, try stay where you are. More you push 'um in deeper, more betta. Make good fertilizer."

David and her cousin Lopaka were in the *lo'i* directly below where Kate was standing. Lopaka was shirtless and wearing his usual baggy surfer shorts, the crotch hanging down almost to his knees. With his dimples and mud-streaked baby face, he looked younger than fifteen. Grinning up at Kate, he was doing an imitation of someone absolutely loving the feel of the mud between his toes.

"*Come!*" Uncle Kimo said to Kate in his most commanding voice. "When you see any green, you stomp 'um down."

Lopaka shook his head and laughed. "She nevah like come. She nevah like get dirty, dats why."

Hating people who laughed at their own stupid jokes, Kate struggled to get her hair inside the clip. She couldn't face the thought of getting mud on her hair.

"Forget it," David said. "She's not gonna do it."

Kate snapped the hair clip, jamming the stray hairs behind her ears. She knelt and then sat with her feet dangling over the bank, her toes touching the muddy water.

Arms folded, Uncle Kimo stood watching as David shook his head, disgusted.

Her loose hair fell forward, sticking to her sweaty cheek. The fierce tropical sun was directly overhead. Perspiration mixed with sunblock burned her eyes.

"Help your sistah," Uncle said, pointing with his chin.

David glanced up, as if deciding whether or not to argue. Then, without a word of protest, he reached out a hand to help Kate into the *lo'i*. She looked for her brother's usual teasing smile. It wasn't there.

"Trust me," he said. "You'll be okay."

The muddy bottom was soft and squishy. She stood clinging to her brother as her feet sank deeper. "What if there are snakes in here?"

"Get no snakes in da Islands," Uncle said. "What you tink, dis da mainland?"

She let go of David's arm and tried to walk. Her feet were sucked deeper into the *lo'i* with each tentative footstep. Lopaka, still smiling his infuriating smile, helped her find a medium-sized weed. "Just work around 'um with your heels," he said, demonstrating.

David smiled encouragement. "Good exercise for ballet. Builds up your calf muscles."

Ignoring the hair plastered to her face, Kate dug in her heels, determined not to give them anything to laugh at. When her weed finally toppled over, David and Lopaka cheered.

"Now you're really getting back to your Hawaiian roots," David said.

How happy he is, Kate thought. She'd never seen her brother so alive. In the weeks they'd been living in Hawai'i, there had actually been moments when he was nice to be around, when he thought about being helpful—the same David who couldn't remember to close the refrigerator door back in California.

Kate kept stepping on her fallen weed until all traces of green disappeared below the surface. Surprisingly, the soft mud felt good under her bare feet. It *was* excellent exercise for a dancer, and she was enjoying the feeling of shared accomplishment.

As her relatives stomped, more and more of the surface was covered with puddles of water instead of weeds. After all the weeds were submerged, the patch would be drained and planted. All the while Uncle was lecturing to one of the younger cousins about how, over the centuries, Hawaiians had learned to cut terraces into the mountains and channel fresh water downhill. "One great engineering feat," he was saying. "Jus' like da pyramids in Egypt!"

Kate had to admit, it was a pretty impressive system. She moved to a bigger weed and began to dig her heels around its base. Minutes later, she had the satisfaction of watching it topple over.

The bottom surface was uneven, and when Kate moved into an adjoining cleared area, she suddenly sank down to her knees in mud, which splashed onto her pink shorts. A second later, she felt herself tottering. She tried to catch herself, desperately grabbing for Lopaka's arm, then lost balance and fell backward.

She flailed with her hands, terrified that her head might sink below the surface, that she would be breathing mud. Finally she gained a footing and managed to stand, mud dripping from her hair, coating her body from the neck down.

"*Ha!*" Lopaka shouted. "She fell on her '*okōle!*"

Uncle was shaking his head. The others just laughed.

I hate them, she thought. *I hate all of them.*

David waded over, wearing his disgusted look again. "They always make a big joke about the first person to fall in. It's only a little mud, so don't overreact," he said. And then, in a softer voice, "Come on. Auntie will get you cleaned up. We're almost finished, anyway."

That evening at the beach Kate sat under a tree and listened to her relatives playing their music, which reminded her of Mehana's beautiful hula. The soft notes flowed around her, mingling with the ocean breeze, and always the lyrics were love songs to the land.

The cove where the Kaheles had their beach picnics looked like a travel poster, the water a perfect turquoise, the beach a perfect white curve. The sun had dipped behind jagged green mountains. Its last rays were almost horizontal, casting long shadows of palm trees across the sand.

Kate looked around at the people—her family. Two cousins were playing ukuleles. Auntie Ruth, the one who was *hāpai*, played guitar. A white-bearded uncle led the three-part harmony. There was a cousin close to her age among the singers. Kate couldn't remember if her name was Kanani or Kalani. She wished she had the courage to go and sit with them.

David and Lopaka and some other cousins were riding the waves as shadows lengthened and the water darkened to purple around them. Kate hadn't really seen her brother surf before. In California they'd lived separate lives. Now it frightened her to watch the ocean rise up behind him and begin to curl down, all those thousands of pounds of water. But when he caught his wave, it was beautiful to watch, like a dance across a constantly shifting surface.

Her father had driven out to join them for dinner. He was sitting at a picnic table with his brother, no doubt arguing. Some aunties gossiped around another table while barefoot children played tag, shrieking with joy. Kate wondered if she should go help clean the tables and wrap up leftovers. But when she'd offered the weekend before, her aunts hadn't seemed to know how to tell her what she could do. They all seemed to work together by some silent code, communicating without words.

So many of the names began with "K"—Keala, Keoni, Kainoa, Kanani, Kalani—she couldn't keep track of who was who. Kate had seen old photos of a *haole* great-grandfather from Scotland who'd jumped ship in Honolulu, but none of them had taken after him. All were dark-haired, their skin colors ranging from Auntie Ruth's light tan to Uncle's burnished mahogany.

Kate shared some of the same genes. She was part of

the same *'ohana*, or extended family. But everything about them was foreign—their language, their laughter, their food. She pretended to eat *poi*. This staple food of the Hawaiians, a purplish mass made from taro root, tasted like sour glue. Worse than the *poi* was a pinkish fish called *lomi* salmon, which was served with it. She'd always hated fish, which was the other favorite Hawaiian food.

Kate knew her father was worried about her, as worried as he could be when he spent all his time worrying about the bar exam. Even her brother must have felt sorry for her after what had happened in the *lo'i*, because he offered to show her how to bodysurf when they got to the beach. But as soon as the first wave broke over her head and she swallowed some water, Kate retreated to the shore. She heard Lopaka say, "Your sistah, she one wimp."

It was true. She was terrified of the ocean. *What's the matter with me?* she asked herself. *A Hawaiian who's afraid of the ocean, who can't stand fish or* poi? *A Hawaiian who would give anything in the world to be back in California.*

Chapter 8

Kate packed away her favorite floppy hat along with her ballet clothes. Her brother took her to a surf shop at Ala Moana Shopping Center, where she bought tank tops and T-shirts, which she wore with shorts or jeans to school. It wasn't a stylish solution to the school clothes problem, but it was safe. Kate blended into the crowd, except for Fridays, when a lot of girls wore *mu'umu'u*, the long dresses that reminded her of nightgowns.

One of the T-shirt logos said NO FEAR, which became a secret joke because Kate spent so much energy trying to look like she wasn't afraid—afraid she'd say the wrong thing, afraid kids would laugh at her and call her *haole*. Each day after school she forced herself to start for home without looking over her shoulder to see if Chad was following her. And she always ran off immediately after the bell to give herself a head start, while Chad was almost always kept behind to finish his work or clean up the mess around his desk.

Even the little things frightened her, the three-inch cockroaches darting across the kitchen floor, the lizards—called "geckos"—that people weren't supposed to kill because they ate cockroaches. Kate went to bed expecting one to fall from the ceiling and land on her in the middle of the night.

Nights were the hardest. She would lie in bed, listening to the dull roar of the freeway, remembering the quiet of home, the smell of eucalyptus from the open window, the down comforter, Boggs snoring quietly at her feet. Most of all, she remembered what it felt like to wake up excited about the coming day. It always took her a long time to fall asleep.

School days fell into a routine that Kate learned to tolerate. In the morning they had math and literature circles. Kate had read most of the novels, but said nothing during discussions. No one noticed her silence; a couple of other kids were also too shy to contribute anything. Recess and lunch, she stayed in the classroom and worked with Jung Hee. Most days, the Korean girl was the only person she would speak to unless Mrs. Odo asked her a question.

Jung Hee knew a lot of math. She just didn't know the names for any of the operations. Sometimes Kate just sat with her and pointed to pictures in a magazine, saying the English words, which the Korean girl would repeat in a timid whisper. Mehana's hula troupe also used the classroom during lunch. Rebecca, the girl who forced Chad to do his math, had clearly danced hula before. For such a large, heavy girl, she was surprisingly graceful. The other volunteers learned the dance quickly with Mehana's patient guidance. Still, they were not all beautiful to watch, although all could do the moves.

This subtle difference among dancers had been true in Kate's ballet troupe back home. Kate wasn't sure you could teach it, much less explain it, this magical thing called "grace." Whatever it was, Mehana had it. Kate loved to watch her move, especially her lovely hands telling their stories.

The song they were dancing to, called "Pua Mana," was about an old house on the island of Maui that was surrounded by flowers and fluttering palm trees. The dancers' fluid movements told of whispering ocean breezes and a round moon rising overhead.

Back at the apartment with her bedroom door locked, Kate practiced the dance. The basic hula move was called a *kaholo*—two steps to the right and then two to the left, the hips swaying in time and marking the rhythm. Watching herself in the mirror, she would add the hand motions, bending her arm like a swaying palm tree or reaching forward to pluck an invisible flower.

Fearful of running into Chad or Richard, Kate always walked home along backstreets. When no one was around, she practiced her hands while she walked, humming the music to "Pua Mana." Soon she knew all the words and movements. During lunchtime practice sessions she would catch Mehana watching her watch them dance.

One afternoon in the second week of practice, Mehana turned to Kate after their first run-through and beckoned. When Kate shrugged her shoulders, pretending she didn't understand, Mehana came over to the classroom library and knelt down on the carpet. "Wouldn't you like to come and dance?" she asked, smiling shyly.

"I've never done hula. I'd just mess you up."

"You know the song. I can see you mouthing the words."

"She know," Jung Hee said, nodding vigorously, her shiny black bangs falling over her eyes.

"Maybe just stand in the back and follow us?" Mehana said.

Kate looked from Mehana's timid, expectant face to Rebecca, who stood in the front line of dancers, hands on her hips. Rebecca had had nothing to say to Kate in the four weeks they'd been in the same classroom. "You like try?" she asked now, as if sensing that some encouragement was needed.

Jung Hee gave Kate's arm a small shove.

Kate stood and handed her the picture book she'd been holding. "I'm not going to be very good," she said. Heart thumping, she went and stood behind the second row of dancers. The music started, and she began to move. She knew from ballet to watch from the corner of her eye and synchronize her movements with the other dancers.

But she didn't need to follow them. She'd been perfecting the palm trees, the moon, and the rolling waves in front of her bedroom mirror.

This is how it feels, Kate thought, remembering, as the music began to flow through her. No one looked at her the first two times they practiced the dance. The third time, Mehana told the dancers she wanted to stand out and watch.

At first Kate was stiff, self-conscious. Forcing herself to breathe deeply, she began to relax and allow her body memory to take over. She felt the moon and the whispering breeze in her pores.

"You really never did hula before?" Mehana asked afterward.

Kate shook her head. "I've done a lot of ballet, though."

That afternoon during social studies, Rebecca picked Kate to be in her group for exploring rain forest issues. Later, Mehana offered to record the hula music if Kate would bring in a blank tape. She seemed to take it for granted that Kate was now part of the hula group.

As soon as she got home, Kate asked her brother to take her to Long's Drug Store to buy a tape. David agreed without grumbling, always happy for an excuse to drive the car.

Their father was staying at the office to study most nights. There wasn't room on the only table for all his books and study guides, and Kate and David had disturbed him whenever they watched the small TV in the bedroom. He would yell at them to turn it down; then they would argue that they couldn't hear it, especially David, who loved to argue almost as much as he loved to eat.

The situation had blown up the week before, when her father stormed into the bedroom and hit the "off" button. "I've told you three times," he yelled. "It's too loud!"

"What are we supposed to do?" David shot back, "They blast the volume on all the commercials!"

"How about homework, Smart Mouth?"

"I'm finished! Even the model student here is finished with her homework!"

Kate didn't bother to say that she never had any homework at Waiala School.

"We're supposed to sit here in silence for the next two months while you study?" David asked. "Is it *our fault* the walls are made of paper?"

Their father took a long, steadying breath. "No, son, it's not your fault. . . . I guess we're all having a tough time adjusting to a small apartment." He looked suddenly guilty. "Can you two handle it if I move my studying to the office?" he asked, and then, to David, "You'd have to stay home nights with your sister. I don't want her left alone."

"Yeah, sure," David said. "My social calendar is pretty clear. I'm bushed after three hours of canoe practice, anyway, and I have to study for the Kamehameha test. Hey, how about if I pick up the car at your office on my way home from school? That way I can help with the shopping and all. I'll just swing by and get you when you're ready to come home."

Their father made a joke about kids with drivers' licenses all of a sudden wanting to do the errands. But Kate couldn't believe her ears. David offering to help with the shopping! David willing to stay home with her!

She suspected part of the personality change was due to Uncle Kimo's lectures on David's responsibility as the *hiapo*, which meant "eldest child." In Hawaiian families, the *hiapo* was supposed to take care of the younger children and help run the house.

As the days passed, David continued to surprise her. Back in California, Mrs. Gomez had done all the cooking. Now that they were on their own, her father said he didn't have time to learn how to cook. He was lucky if he had time to eat. Uncle Kimo—with a faultfinding look at his younger brother—had told David it was "no shame" for a man to do the cooking.

With lessons from Uncle and a few disasters, David perfected Uncle Kimo's stew, the gravy thickened with taro and served over rice the Hawaiian way. Her brother also liked inventing what their father called "creative salads," because David experimented with strange-looking lettuce and weird combinations, like walnuts and papaya with slices of hot dog.

Kate's kitchen job was to cut up vegetables or grate the cooked taro. When they got tired of Hawaiian stew, they would call out for pizza or Auntie would send salmon and *poi* or another dish called *lau lau*, made of pork and fish wrapped in *ti* leaves. Those nights Kate had cereal and toast for dinner. It was a world away from Mrs. Gomez's wonderful Mexican cooking.

Still, whenever Kate played the "Pua Mana" tape Mehana had made for her, the world didn't seem quite so bleak. She would move around the kitchen, humming the words and dancing with her hands. The music was moving through her, filling an emptiness she hadn't known was so deep. She wondered if she could ask Mehana to record some other dances so she could learn them, too.

Chapter 9

*K*ate got her wish. Their hula group was doing so well that Mehana got permission to teach them a second dance for the talent show. The new one was a *kahiko*, or ancient hula, and it was very different from the fluid hands and gliding hips in "Pua Mana."

Mehana explained that this was the way hula used to be danced, when people from other Polynesian islands had first settled in Hawai'i. Some dances were exactly the same as they'd been performed hundreds of years ago. The dancers' arms extended straight out, with locked wrists and fingers pressed tightly together. Instead of guitar and ukulele accompaniment, a hollow gourd sounded the rhythm. The words, chanted from deep inside the throat, sounded like something between song and prayer.

The chanter on the tape was Mehana's hula teacher, a woman called Kumu Kalama. Her hula troupe, or *halau*, which regularly won statewide hula competitions, was very strict. If Mehana missed a practice, she had to write an essay explaining her absence and describing her goals as a dancer. Kate wondered if there were any *haoles* or even *hapa haoles* like herself in the *halau*. But she was afraid to ask Mehana, especially after what happened in class one morning.

Rebecca and Mehana were both in Kate's literature circle, reading a novel called *My Side of the Mountain*. There was a question on their study sheet about a character nicknamed "Thoreau," a boy in the story who'd gone to live alone in the woods.

No one could figure out why the boy had gotten that nickname, and without thinking, Kate jumped into the conversation. "There was a writer named Thoreau, back in the eighteen hundreds," she said. "Just like the kid in the story. He—the writer Thoreau—went to live in the woods. In this cabin on a lake, a pond, really. . . ." She caught Rebecca's stare and finished lamely, "He wanted to get away from civilization."

Almost as soon as the words were out of her mouth, Kate knew she'd made a mistake. David had been warning her to be careful about sounding too smart. The other students must have thought she was showing off instead of helping to answer the question on the study sheet.

She should have known. Just because these girls allowed her to dance with them, it didn't mean they were her friends. They weren't her friends. They would never be able to accept who she was—a person who'd gone to an excellent school, who happened to have read a lot of books.

Another day in math class Kate managed to get in trouble by knowing the answer even when she was trying not to. Mrs. Odo was telling the class what exponents were when she caught Kate's eye. "I'm sure Kathryn can explain," she said, smiling.

Kate shook her head, her face growing hot.

"Go ahead, *haole* girl," Chad sneered. "Show us how smart you are. How perfect you can talk."

"Certain people in this room would be a lot smarter if they took school more seriously," Mrs. Odo said to him, and then to Kate, "Can you come up to the board and show the class what eight to the second power means . . . ?"

It was the awful silence pooling around her that propelled Kate from her seat. Up at the board, heart pounding in her ears, she wrote out the solution and then retreated to her pod, turning her back on Chad's smirk. Kate made up her mind to keep her mouth shut and her eyes downcast whenever Mrs. Odo was up at the board. She couldn't let down her guard, not even with Mehana.

She was surprised, then, on the day of the dress rehearsal for the talent show, when Mehana brought up the hula *halau* on her own. They were sitting on the carpet in the classroom library, sewing long, pointed *ti* leaves onto cotton waistbands to make their hula skirts. Jung Hee was helping them sew. The other girls were off picking flowers to string into leis.

"Did you ever think about joining a *halau*?" Mehana asked, without looking up. "I could maybe introduce you to my teacher, Kumu Kalama."

"You *could*?" Kate was embarrassed to ask how much hula lessons would cost. Her father had said he would find money for her to continue ballet, but in the past month he'd forgotten about his promise. They'd had no offers for the house in California, and her father wouldn't be paid by HARA until he was an official lawyer in the state of Hawai'i. Of course, he couldn't become an official lawyer until he passed the bar exam. If he didn't pass, they would have to take charity from Uncle Kimo, which was probably why he was studying so hard.

That night she was waiting for her father when he came through the door, looking more exhausted than usual.

"Dad," she said, "Mehana wants me to try out for her hula *halau*."

He set down his briefcase and lowered himself onto the couch.

"Mehana. You know, the one who's teaching us for the talent show?"

"The talent show! When did you say that was?"

"It's tomorrow. At one-thirty."

"*No!* We'll be meeting at the legislature all afternoon. Kimo's group is planning a march on 'Iolani Palace, to protest the overthrow of the Hawaiian Kingdom. I'm trying to get official permission so we can avoid a scuffle with the police. . . ." He looked up, massaging his brow.

"It's all right," she lied, "I don't think many parents will be there, anyway."

"I'm really sorry."

"Dad, I have a chance to join Mehana's *halau*." She decided not to say anything about the money. "They won the Merrie Monarch Festival year before last. Can I?"

"Sure, sounds great."

"They practice at Washington School's cafeteria. Thursday afternoons at four-thirty. I can walk there. Mehana's uncle will pick us up afterward."

"Okay, fine," he said, and then, as she was going into the kitchen, "Honey, I'm sorry about the talent show. Things'll be different when I get this exam out of the way."

The morning of the show, putting on her costume and makeup, Kate found herself missing her ballet friends back home. But it felt good, too, being part of a group, all dressed the same, all talking about how nervous they were.

When the time came to perform, she forgot her nervousness. She forgot everything except the music and the dance and the audience out in front. She even remembered to smile during the modern hula and to keep her face serious during the *kahiko*, when dancers weren't supposed to smile.

Their group was voted first place in the talent competition. Mrs. Odo had hugs for all of them, and several girls from her literature circle told Kate she was a good dancer. But this feeling of belonging lasted only until the refreshments were served.

Kate, still in her *ti*-leaf skirt and yellow camisole, was helping herself to a doughnut when she noticed Chad at the next table. He had a Coke can and was shaking it vigorously. She prayed he would leave her alone, now that she'd proved herself capable of dancing hula.

"What, boddah you?" he demanded, catching her eye.

Kate couldn't understand the question.

He swaggered over, threatening to pull the tab on the Coke and spray the contents all over her. "You tink you one Hawaiian now?"

Richard, who was never far away, joined in the attack. "She not Hawaiian. She *hāpai!* Cannot dance, she too pregnant."

Kate glanced over her shoulder to see if any of the other dancers were in sight. Her exit was blocked by Chad and Richard and a couple of girls who hung around with them. She could hear Uncle's voice saying, "*She gotta get more tough.*"

"I don't know what I ever did to you," she said. "Just leave me alone, and I'll leave you alone, okay?"

"My sistah," Chad sneered. "She going beat da shit outta you."

Kate stood her ground. "I don't even know your sister." Her mouth felt dry. She could feel her bottom lip starting to tremble.

"I tell her get you, she get you," Chad said, thrusting his face next to hers. "She come with her gang from McKauley High School. Dey all hate *haoles,* jus' like me."

Kate sprinted away as soon as school was dismissed. She told herself she could keep out of his way because there was always some assignment he needed to stay and finish. She told herself he was probably all talk. She fought back the panic.

The next day she rode her bike to school to give her an even better edge. She didn't tell anyone about Chad's threat. Her father would want to move her to another school, just when she maybe had some friends at this one. Her brother would tell her she needed to learn how to fight back.

She didn't want to fight back. She didn't want to think about why Chad hated her, why a sister who'd never even seen her would want to beat her up. More than anything, she wanted some people she could belong with. She wanted something to look forward to when she woke up in the morning. Mehana's hula *halau* could give her that. She wasn't going to spoil her chance to be a part of it, not for anything.

On Thursday afternoon she asked David for a ride to hula practice. She would have had to pass near Chad's sister's school on her way to Washington Intermediate, where Mehana's *halau* met. Even as she calculated how to avoid him, Kate was disgusted with herself for letting Chad make her so afraid.

"Good thing I have the car," David said on their way to practice. "I'm gonna pick up Dad at nine. Get him to come home for a night's sleep."

Kate didn't want to worry about her father; she was too busy worrying about herself. Would she have to dance "Pua Mana" for Kumu Kalama to see if she was good enough for the *halau*? *Would* she be good enough? Rebecca was in the *halau*, and she wasn't nearly as good a dancer as Mehana.

David said, "Dad's so stressed about the exam. Worse than when he was getting ready for a big case back in California."

Kate remembered those times when they'd hardly seen their father for weeks at a time. At least there had been Mrs. Gomez and the Lindseys and her ballet classes.

"Then there's the latest with Uncle Kimo," David was saying. "Uncle's insisting we give up the apartment and move in with him. He says we're latchkey kids, that Dad doesn't have time to take care of us, and that's not the Hawaiian way." He glanced at Kate's expression of dismay. "Don't worry, that's not gonna happen. It makes Dad fighting mad when Uncle—the *hiapo*—starts ordering him around. Besides, I don't want to change schools, not unless I get into Kamehameha. The canoe *hale* is five minutes from our apartment.

You should see the awesome chicks that hang around there."

Kate sighed. "Remember how Dad was supposed to have more time to spend with us after the big lifestyle change?"

"At least in California he'd take us on trips after he won a big case," David said. "Remember the dude ranch?"

"Yeah, that was fun," she said, and after a silence, "Dad and Uncle Kimo are fighting about some kind of demonstration?"

"Uncle's got this plan to march on 'Iolani Palace. It's part of the hundred-year anniversary of the overthrow. All the sovereignty groups camping out with their tents on the palace lawn. Dad wants to get a permit to occupy the palace grounds. But Uncle Kimo doesn't agree. He *wants* to get arrested!"

"What for?"

"Publicity. Uncle wants a media event. The United States government throwing Hawaiians in jail. Picture it on CNN. Children with flowers in their hair, old ladies chanting. Uncle says Dad will be letting down his people if he refuses to go to jail with them. But Dad can't go to jail. He won't be accepted by the Hawai'i Bar Association if he has any police record. They'll be checking all the way back to high school."

David pulled the car into the Washington School parking lot. "Is this the place?"

Kate saw Mehana sitting on the steps. "Over there,"

she said. "You don't have to pick me up. Mehana's uncle is driving me home."

Without looking back, she ran across the parking lot to join Mehana. It felt good to leave her family's problems behind and go lose herself in dance.

Chapter 10

*T*he woman on the cafeteria stage reminded Kate of the portraits of ali'i, the Hawaiian nobility, in David's history book. Kumu Kalama was at least six feet tall. Her glossy black hair was drawn into a twist, and she wore a white ginger lei and a blue *mu'umu'u* that fell in a train at her bare feet. In California she might have been called fat. But that was not a word Kate would have used to describe her. She had what Hawaiians called *mana*. It meant spiritual power, a kind of inner strength people were drawn to. Mehana had explained that *kumu* was the Hawaiian word for teacher, and that hula teachers commanded a lot of respect.

Kate needn't have worried about having to try out. When Mehana brought her up onstage to introduce her, Kumu scarcely nodded in Kate's direction before waving her into the back row of dancers and then calling the class to order.

Mehana took her place in the front row, glancing over her shoulder with an encouraging smile. The twenty or so other girls who'd been milling around quickly found their places. Some looked younger than Kate and Mehana. Several, like Rebecca, looked older. The girls all had long dark hair that swayed gracefully when they moved their hips—so different from ballerinas, who pulled their hair into tight buns so that it wouldn't detract from the dance.

Mehana's group was learning a modern hula called "Ke Awāwa" about a remote valley on the island of Moloka'i.

"Moloka'i is one of our last frontiers," Kumu told them. "There are still sacred places there, and this song is about one of them. Before the white man came, there were maybe half a million Hawaiians living on these islands. Some say a million. But the *haole* brought diseases, and our people had no immunity. Now the valley is almost empty of people. Disease, oppression, hopelessness have wiped them out. This song is asking them to come back."

Kumu translated each verse into English and demonstrated the movements. In the song's chorus the valley itself was calling the people back: "Come home to the fragrant land. . . ." Kate loved the poetry of the words. Fascinated by Kumu's hands beckoning to the valley's lost inhabitants, she did her best to imitate the movements.

At the end of the hour Kumu Kalama said nothing about whether Kate could come back again, and Mehana seemed afraid to ask. Just as they were leaving the cafeteria, Kumu called after them, "Mehana, teach your friend the practice tape. She should know the steps by next Thursday."

Over the next week during lunch and recess, Mehana taught Kate the steps she hadn't yet learned and helped her polish the ones she already knew. With *kaholo*, the basic step, Kate had been sliding her feet to the right and left instead of lifting and placing them. They also worked on the fine points in "Ke Awāwa"—the facial expressions, the curve of the hands—and on synchronizing their movements so that one dancer seemed a shadow of the other. Sometimes Rebecca joined them, but most days she ran off to play tetherball.

Mehana made Kate a copy of the practice tape, which included all the steps in both ancient and modern hula, with Kumu Kalama chanting the changes in her deep, resonant voice. At home, Kate practiced it over and over again. Afterward, she felt a pleasant ache in her thighs that reminded her of evenings after ballet classes back in California.

On Wednesday, the day before hula class, Mehana suggested that they stay after school for a final practice. Kate didn't want to hang around with Chad at large, but she didn't want to tell that to Mehana. "Can you come to my house?" she asked. "It's not very big, but we can push back the furniture in the living room."

"Sure, that's better than my house," Mehana said. "I

have three little brothers all over the living room floor. They can't be pushed back."

After school Kate walked her bike with Mehana walking beside her. Mehana, usually shy and quiet, talked easily about her family, a single mom and three brothers she often had to baby-sit. Uncle Ray, the one who'd picked them up after hula, wasn't really an uncle. He was her mother's boyfriend. Mehana said, "He's a lot better than the last one. He gets us videos, makes popcorn. I think maybe they'll get married.

"This is great!" Mehana exclaimed when they opened the door to Kate's apartment. "Check out this view of Diamond Head! Just like the postcards!"

What kind of house did Mehana have, Kate wondered, if she thought this tiny apartment with its fake-wood furniture and brown carpeting was nice. Or was she just being polite?

"Does your mother work?" Mehana asked.

"She died . . . when I was little." Kate hated having to explain about her mother. People always looked at her with such pity in their eyes. "I don't really remember her," she said. "It was so long ago."

"My mother and father are divorced. Except he doesn't come around much. He's got a new wife and a baby."

Mehana went out onto the *lānai* and stood, elbows on the rail, admiring the view. The breeze lifted her hair, the sun burnishing it with bronze highlights. "You must be close to your aunties," she said. "Are they the ones who took care of you?"

"I didn't even know my aunts till I moved here after Christmas. There was just me and my father and brother. And our dog, Boggs. We had a housekeeper who did the cooking and cleaned the house. Mrs. Gomez. I really miss her." Turning away, Kate pushed the coffee table up against the couch. "Ready to dance?"

They went through "Ke Awāwa" several times and then reviewed both hulas from the talent show. When David came home from canoe practice, he flopped onto the couch, eating popcorn, and watched them do all three dances again.

"You should both be dancing down in the hotels!" he said. "I'm impressed."

Mehana smiled shyly.

"Your brother's nice," Mehana said when Kate was taking her down in the elevator. "Cute, too! Does he have a girlfriend?"

"Two different girls are calling him up, one from school and one from canoeing."

"He paddles down at the Ala Wai Canal?"

"For Waikīkī Surf Club. He got roped into it by our uncle, who's a big deal in the club. Uncle Kimo's always making speeches about how Hawaiian outrigger canoes used to travel all over the Pacific centuries before Columbus. . . ."

"So which girl does he like?"

"He's not really dating either one. If I know David, he's probably trying to keep both of them guessing. Anyway," Kate said, smiling, "he's too old for you."

Mehana blushed. "How old *is* he?"

"Sixteen."

"He seems a lot older."

"Since we moved to Hawai'i, it's like he grew up overnight. He's reading books about Hawaiian history, telling me stories about the kings and queens. He *never* used to read. All of a sudden, he wants to be a lawyer and specialize in Hawaiian land rights. We're both supposed to be taking the entrance test for Kamehameha School. He's actually studying for it."

"In April? Me, too! I'll be okay on the verbal sections. I'm worried about the math part, though."

"David's worried about the math, too. He's not dumb or anything. He just never paid much attention to school. Now he doesn't even know simple things like fractions."

Mehana laughed. "Whenever anybody says 'common denominator,' I get all jammed up. . . ." She stood a moment, holding on to the lobby door. "Maybe you could help me like you help Jung Hee? You know the study guide for the test? My mother knows how to do the problems, but she can't explain it."

"Sure, we can work on it at lunch." Kate didn't tell Mehana she'd been in a special advanced math class back home, that she was already helping her brother with the test's study guide.

"I can use the practice, too," Kate said. "Jung Hee is actually a whiz at math. She'll wind up helping us both."

*　　*　　*

At Thursday's hula class Kate knew "Ke Awāwa" perfectly. At the end of the song, Kumu Kalama nodded approvingly, and she felt a rush of pride. When the *halau* started learning a *kahiko* hula that was faster than anything Kate had done so far, she was able to keep up. At the end of session, Kumu told her she should come Saturday mornings as well as Thursday afternoons.

"What do I have to pay for the lessons?" she asked Mehana when they were sitting on the steps waiting for Uncle Ray to pick them up.

"Pay?" Mehana looked puzzled. "We don't pay anything to learn the dances. They belong to everyone. Oh, we have to dance sometimes when Kumu puts on a show down in Waikīkī. I think maybe she gets paid for that."

Kate thought about how much ballet lessons had cost back home and then remembered something Uncle had said, that the Hawaiians were in such bad shape because they always gave away everything they owned.

For the next two weeks Kate lived hula, and no longer in the privacy of her room. She danced her way down the hall, she would *kaholo* around the kitchen, always working to imitate the fluid hand movements of Mehana and Kumu Kalama.

Whenever David passed her in the hallway, he would sing out, "'Lovely hula hands,'" the chorus from an old Hawaiian song. If he was home, her father would look up from his books and smile.

There was an added benefit to joining the *halau*. The

Saturday morning practice would keep Kate out of the taro patch. Even Uncle Kimo couldn't object to that excuse.

At night she would move her hands in the beautiful gestures and watch the shadows on the wall, searching for Kumu's effortless grace. When she lay in bed, the Hawaiian music was still flowing through her, its rhythm keeping time with her heartbeat, making her feel less lonely.

Chapter 11

At their next family *lu'au* Kate managed to have a conversation with Auntie Alohi, who wanted to know all about the *halau*, which dances Kate had learned, which style of choreography. Two other aunties were sharing their own hula memories. Auntie Ruth, whose pregnancy was starting to show, was at the big kitchen table, laughing and telling about her mother-in-law's *halau*, which was for women who weighed more than two hundred pounds.

"*Mai poina*, no forget," Uncle interrupted. "Da gods taught us how to dance. Hula had *mana*." He stooped to retrieve a container of chicken from the refrigerator. "Used to *consecrate* dancers before performance. Dancers stay fasting. Now dey wearing plastic skirts. Entertaining tourists."

After he'd gone back outside, Auntie Alohi said to Kate, "Don't listen to him. What is it you say? His growl is worse than his bite?"

Kate looked up in surprise. Imagine not listening to Uncle Kimo. "His *bark* is worse than his bite," she said, smiling.

"He's really touched, here"—Auntie Alohi put her hand on her heart—"that you are learning our dances."

"Then what's he so mad at?"

Auntie Ruth laughed. "Because Kimo one hard-headed buggah, right, Auntie?"

Auntie Alohi said, "Uncle needs to be sure it's *pono*—what's the word in English?—that it's proper. That it's a . . . serious *halau* you're joining. When he hears that Puanani Kalama is your *kumu*, Uncle will be very proud. And with the dance will come the language," she added after a silence.

"You mean Pidgin?"

"Not Pidgin; you'll learn that, anyway, from the other kids. I mean Hawaiian, *Ka ʻolelo makuahine*, the mother tongue."

Auntie Alohi moved to the kitchen table to help Auntie Ruth and another auntie who were wrapping pork and fish in *ti* leaves to make *lau lau*. Kate watched them fill the leaves and then double-wrap each one with two larger leaves, folded crosswise. After she finished the lettuce, Kate went over and picked up a leaf herself. Imitating her aunts, she put some of the filling inside and tried to make the folds.

Auntie Ruth showed her how to pull loose a strand from the stem to tie up the small green packet. Kate began another *lau lau*. She didn't much like the way they tasted, but it was fun making them.

She was beginning to understand how her relatives worked together. No matter how big a party they were preparing food for, there was very little explaining about what needed to be done. You watched what was going on and then picked up a knife and started chopping taro or onions. If you weren't cutting the right size, someone would come along and demonstrate. It was so different from the way Mrs. Lindsey was always talking, always explaining things to Kate and Sara when they helped in the kitchen.

When her cousin Lopaka and Ruth's husband, Kainoa, came and joined them at the table, Lopaka looked surprised to see Kate helping. "Pretty good—for one *haole*," he said, picking up the *lau lau* Kate had just finished tying.

Auntie Alohi fixed him with a stern look.

"Just kidding, mom."

"*Pa'a ka waha, hana nā, lima,*" she said, and then translated. "Work with the hands, not the mouth. Hawaiians are forgetting the power of silence."

Lopaka began filling one of the *ti* leaves. Another uncle joined them at the kitchen table, and they all worked together without a word. After a while Auntie Ruth began to sing in her clear, rich voice. It was a song about making a lei for Lili'uokalani, the last Hawaiian queen, the one the Americans had locked up in her own palace. They all knew the words and joined in the three-part harmony that Hawaiians seemed to be born knowing. By the end Kate was able to sing along on the chorus. It was a beautiful melody, but it sounded sad, too. A hundred years had passed since the overthrow of the Hawaiian Kingdom, but the family still seemed really sad about what had happened to poor Lili'uokalani.

Kate wished she knew what the words were saying about this doomed queen who had been Hawai'i's last monarch. She knew from her brother's history book that when the U.S. Marines marched in, Lili'uokalani had refused to allow the Hawaiians to fight back, because she didn't want any of her people to get hurt.

When Kate carried the first tray of *lau lau* out to the *lānai*, she was beginning to feel some connection to this *'ohana*. It was the first time she hadn't felt like a visitor from another planet.

Some people were gathered around the grill drinking beer. Uncle Kimo was sounding off about the public schools. "Hawaiian language should be one *requirement!*" he was insisting. "Schools gotta be reorganized according to *Hawaiian* values!"

"Before that can happen, we have to produce more Hawaiian teachers," Kate's father said.

"True," said Pele, a cousin who taught math at the local high school. "Even out here, with our mostly Hawaiian population, we're still a minority in the teaching profession."

Uncle shook his head in disgust. "Get too many Japanese teachers telling Hawaiian kids dey no good.

How dey gonna learn when teachers all time telling dem dey stupid?"

Kimo was right about one thing. Kate had noticed that almost all the teachers at her school were of Japanese ancestry, like Mrs. Odo. But he was wrong about how they treated Hawaiian kids—or any kids. Kate didn't know if Chad was Hawaiian, but she always marveled at how Mrs. Odo could stay so cheerful and patient with him. Even keeping him after school to finish his work was because she cared about him. And she never did it in a mean way.

"I have a Japanese teacher," Kate heard herself say. "Mrs. Odo. Japanese American, really. She's the nicest teacher I ever had. She doesn't make Hawaiian kids—or any kids—feel stupid. . . ."

She caught sight of Auntie Alohi's half smile. Could her aunt be encouraging her to speak up?

"You can't say all Japanese teachers are bad," Kate rushed on. "You're doing the same thing people used to do to Hawaiians, lumping you all together. Like you're all stupid because you're Hawaiians. . . ."

"It's called stereotyping," the math teacher cousin said, smiling.

Kate's father was smiling, too.

"Wisdom from a child," said Auntie Alohi.

Uncle Kimo took the tray from Kate, shaking his head. "Some of dese *lau lau* not folded right," he said.

Kate breathed a sigh of relief. Her aunt was smiling. Her father was smiling. There wasn't going to be a fight.

But the good mood lasted only until dinner. As they sat listening to the sudden afternoon rain on the *lānai*'s tin roof, talk turned to the march on 'Iolani Palace.

"HARA sent a written request on Friday," her father said. "We're hoping they'll issue permits for us to camp out on the palace grounds."

Uncle Kimo's expression darkened. He didn't say anything, just exchanged a knowing look with Auntie Ruth's husband. But in that second there was a shift of mood. Kate looked around at the faces at the long table. She didn't know which of the relatives were on Uncle Kimo's side, in the sovereignty group that wanted to get arrested, and which ones agreed with her father.

And she didn't want to know. She didn't want to hear about marches and sovereignty and Hawaiian values, whatever they were. Why couldn't Auntie Ruth just start another song? Why did everything with Hawaiians have to turn serious? Even hula had to be serious, *pono*.

They finished eating dinner without an argument, but Kate could feel the tension, even if nobody talked about the march. Dessert was a coconut pudding called *haupia*, the only Hawaiian food Kate really liked. But she didn't get to have any. When they were clearing off the dinner dishes, her father announced that they had to leave, that he'd been away from his books for too long.

On the ride back home, David asked, "Do you think Uncle will find some other way to get arrested—even if you do get the permit?"

Their father was quiet a moment. "I don't know. It's

impossible to talk to him." His hands tightened on the steering wheel as he stared out into the tropic dusk. "Another happy *lu'au* with the family all together," he said, frowning into the windshield.

Chapter 12

"My dad sending you some *haupia*," cousin Lopaka said, sliding a plastic container across the kitchen counter where Kate stood at the sink doing dishes.

Kate glanced at the container and then at her cousin, who had just breezed into their apartment carrying one of the care packages of food that Auntie Alohi regularly provided. "*Haupia?* That's great!" she said, and then added, "Really? From Uncle Kimo?"

Hands in the pockets of his baggy shorts, Lopaka shrugged. "Dad tell Mom, 'Get one Tupperware. We send dat girl some *haupia*. Only ting she evah eats. . . .'"

Kate wiped dishwater off her hands and picked up the container, fingering it with wonder. She wouldn't have expected Uncle Kimo to even notice what she ate.

Lopaka said, "Remember you guys had to leave early? Didn't get dessert. Auntie Ruth's brownies in dat other bag. And some of dat *lau lau* you made." He grinned. "Looks pretty *hemmejang* but tastes okay."

"Thanks," Kate murmured as Lopaka sauntered off toward David's room.

"Hey, Kaleo!" he yelled. "Mario's waiting. Parked in one loading zone!"

Her father came into the kitchen carrying the rest of the dinner dishes. "Where are they going?" he asked.

"Paddling. Time trials. With the cousins and their friend."

"Who's driving?"

"Mario, the big guy. Football player."

"Okay. Now I remember. Seems like a responsible kid. I didn't want to hurt David's feelings," he said, scraping the remains of his salad into the garbage, "but this latest is too creative for me. Anchovies, ugh!"

Her father stacked plates in the dishpan and ran hot water on them. "Can you take care of these, Katey girl? I have to go back to the office."

"Sure. What does *hemmejang* mean?"

"It means sort of . . . messed up. Why, what was *hemmejang?*"

"The *lau lau* I made with Auntie last weekend. At least that's what Lopaka says about them."

Her father laughed. "Next time you can say back, *'What, boddah you?'* English translation: 'Pardon me, does that bother you?' Say it tough and sarcastic, local style."

"What, boddah you?" Kate said, overdoing the Pidgin accent and shoving her hands into the pockets of her jeans to imitate her cousin's favorite surfer pose.

"By George, she's got it!"

"Dad, you're picking me up tonight at Mehana's house. You didn't forget that, did you?"

"No, I didn't forget. You've got a meeting of the full *halau*. A big deal. Mehana's uncle—who's really her mother's boyfriend—is picking you up afterward and you're going back home with them. See? Memory like a steel trap." He flicked the dish towel at her. "I even remember that you're going away this weekend with the *halau*."

"Not this weekend. The one after. To get ready for the palace march. A lot of *halau* will be dancing on the palace grounds. Kumu Kalama's very fussy about how we're gonna look. Worse than Madame Briansky back home. TV news will be there filming."

"I know. The same cameras my brother hopes will be on us being dragged off to jail by an oppressive American government." He sighed, his smile fading. "Let's not talk about it. I need to go immerse myself in property law and some other trivia I haven't looked at since law school."

"Think you'll be ready?"

"Who knows? Exam starts the week after the march. I don't want to think about either one. You're walking to Washington School?"

She had been planning to ask for a ride. But it was still full daylight. Why should she let Chad make her afraid to walk the streets?

"Sure," she said, standing on tiptoe to give him a kiss.

Her father's happy mood had disappeared. Whenever he talked about the bar exam or about his brother, Kimo, the same troubled look came back into his eyes.

All the classes in the *halau Nā Pua a Kapo* were at the meeting, filling the benches in the cafeteria. Kate sat in between Mehana and Rebecca, across from some adorable kids from the *keiki*, or children's, hula group. Many had mothers or aunties in the adult women's group. A dozen or so teenage boys and young men stood nearby. Their lean, athletic bodies reminded Kate of the male dancers in her ballet troupe back home.

For Uncle Kimo's two-day protest at 'Iolani Palace, all Kumu Kalama's classes would be dancing one hula together, a *kahiko*, an ancient-style hula written about Hawaiian sovereignty. This would be the finale for the whole weekend, and their *halau* was honored to have been chosen to dance it. For their entry onto the stage, they would be reciting a chant Kumu Kalama had written about opening the way to sovereignty.

Kumu passed out papers with the Hawaiian lyrics and went over them, word by word. They repeated after her until they had the correct pronunciation. Then she taught them how to clap their hands in a complicated beat as they walked.

"I can't get away from this sovereignty thing," Kate said later to Mehana. "Even my brother has an opinion. He's bummed because he'll be too young to vote in the special election about it."

Mehana looked at her thoughtfully. "I don't even know what sovereignty's supposed to be like."

"That's what my family's arguing about. The people my father works for think we should still be in the United States but have some parts of the different islands just run by Hawaiians. Like the Indians on the mainland run their own reservations. But my uncle's group wants the whole state back for Hawaiians, a separate nation like they were before. I'm not sure what would happen to everyone else. . . ."

"Uncle Ray's from the Philippines. I don't want him to have to leave."

"Don't worry. My dad says Uncle's group would be voted down, that they're scaring people away from sovereignty."

On Thursday Kate walked again to Washington School for hula practice. She saw no sign of Chad and made up her mind to stop worrying about him. *If he even looks my way*, she promised herself, *I'll just stick my hands into my pockets and say, "What, boddah you?"*

But Chad's next move caught her completely off guard. At the end of recess, Mrs. Odo had sent Kate to the girls' bathroom to fill a pitcher with water for the classroom geraniums. As she walked back to the room, Chad came running from behind and slammed her into the cement wall. The plastic pitcher clattered to the ground, water splashing all over her feet. For a second Kate didn't know what had happened. She just stood there watching Chad run away, his laughter ringing in her ears.

"She drop da pitcher, poor ting," came Richard's voice from behind.

That afternoon Kate stood at her bedroom mirror, studying a purplish bruise that almost covered her upper arm. Her brother was right; she'd led a sheltered life. She tried to imagine a girl pushing another student into a cement wall at Saint Theresa's and gave up. It was unimaginable.

When her brother came home, she rolled up her sleeve and showed him the bruise.

His first reaction was anger—at her. "You gotta hit back. I keep telling you."

"I can't!"

"Look, Kate. It's not a perfect world. Kids hit each other. . . ." He took a breath, as if willing himself to be patient. "Did you tell your teacher?"

She shook her head. All afternoon she had sat in her pod in dazed silence.

"So, okay." David got up from the couch and paced over to the window. "That's what you do, tell your teacher. There has to be some kind of counselor who could talk to him. . . ."

"Why does Chad hate me so much? Hawai'i's supposed to be 'the Aloha State,' where all races live together in harmony. What a joke!"

David sighed. "Some *haole* plantation owners stole a

kingdom from the Hawaiians. The American government supported them, too. Other races—Chinese, Japanese, Filipino—they lived like slaves on those same plantations. There's a lot of bad blood, even now."

"*I* didn't do any of those things! Besides, I'm as Hawaiian as you! It's not fair!"

"It doesn't *have* to be fair! Who said anything had to be fair?"

She swallowed, willing herself not to cry, sure her brother would see tears as another sign of weakness. "I'm sorry I'm such a disappointment," she whispered.

David shook his head in frustration. "Listen, let's not tell Dad. Not now, anyway. He's already so freaked over the exam. This morning he drove right through a red light. Fighting with Uncle about the damn march."

Kate felt her bottom lip tremble, and David looked away. "It's no big deal for one kid to push another kid at school," he said. "Boys play rough. Just talk to your teacher tomorrow morning."

She nodded and turned away. It wasn't any casual push. Chad wanted to hurt her, of that she was sure. But her brother didn't want to hear about it.

"Keep your sleeve down. Don't let Dad see your arm," he called after her as she retreated to her room.

The next morning, when Kate arrived at school, a substitute teacher was behind Mrs. Odo's desk. David's plan would have to be postponed. Even worse, there would be no one to keep Chad after school and give her a head start out of the neighborhood.

"I usually stay in during recess," she explained to Mr. King, the substitute, her voice sounding strange in her ears. "Some of us work on our math and clean up the room."

He looked up from some papers. "I'm supposed to shoo you out and lock the door. Come on, some fresh air will do you good."

"Let's go to the library," Mehana suggested. "You and Jung Hee can check my math. I did the section on dividing fractions and I think they're okay. You're a good teacher!"

To Kate's relief, Chad ran off to the playground with Richard. She was beginning to think the day would go by without any problems. But right after lunch he started tearing around the classroom, making people laugh. When he dashed by Kate's table, he stuck out his arm and swept her books off her desk, scattering papers onto the floor.

Mehana knelt to help pick them up. "He acts like such a retard!" Kate said under her breath. She regretted the words almost at once, because Chad had heard. She'd only made him angrier.

"Stupid *haole!*" Chad yelled back. "*You* the retard!"

The substitute couldn't get him to sit down. He had to call the principal, Mr. Matsumoto, who came and took Chad to his office. After Chad came back to the room, he sat slumped down in his seat, arms crossed, fuming quietly. Even Rebecca couldn't get him to do any work.

When they moved into their social studies groups, Chad came over to Kate's table and leaned down, speaking softly, "Me and Richard waiting for you after school. Get my sister and her gang. We know where you live."

The last hour seemed endless. Kate couldn't think clearly about what to do. Should she tell Mehana? David was right, kids got pushed and threatened at school. It happened all the time. And Mehana was shy, but she didn't put up with any of Chad's abuse. Would she still want to be Kate's friend if she knew what a wimp she was?

Kate passed her a note during free reading: WANT TO COME HOME WITH ME AFTER SCHOOL?

"Can't," Mehana whispered. "I'm leaving right away. My mom's picking me up."

Kate considered telling Rebecca. But Rebecca seemed just to tolerate her presence at hula. Kate wasn't sure if Rebecca would protect her or join Chad and his sister's gang.

She thought of going to the nurse's office and saying she was sick. They would have to call her father to come get her. She actually did feel sick to her stomach, but she was too paralyzed to tell the substitute.

The minutes ticked on. Whenever she looked over at his pod, Chad was staring at her, giving her stink eye. *Don't cry*, she said to herself. *Don't let him see you cry.* She kept thinking about the kid Chad had supposedly beat up down at Waikīkī—a tourist staying with his family at one of the hotels.

What would his sister's gang do to her? Hit her with their fists? Pull hair? Throw rocks? Or would it be worse? Would one of them, maybe Chad, have a knife? In her mind's eye, Kate ran a tape of a TV news clip on gang violence, kids running away and a stabbed victim, her blood seeping onto the pavement.

She felt a wave of nausea. As soon as the dismissal bell rang, she raced to the toilet, but couldn't throw up. At the public telephone she dialed her father's office with shaking hands. He wasn't in, and there was no way to get in touch with David at the high school.

Next she ran back to the class lockers, determined to find Rebecca and tell her what was happening. But no one was around; the substitute had already locked up the room.

With a pulse pounding in her ears, Kate wheeled her bike out of the school parking area. Chad and Richard were nowhere in sight. In fact, the whole neighborhood seemed deserted. The afternoon had clouded over, with a cool breeze sweeping off the ocean. Still, her skin had broken out in a mist of perspiration. She shivered, fighting down another wave of nausea.

She climbed onto her bike. As she began to pedal, she could hear her uncle's voice saying, *"She jus' needs to get more tough."*

Chapter 13

Kate followed her usual route along the back-streets, praying they wouldn't look for her there. There was no one around. She kept thinking about the young tourist down in Waikīkī. Had he tried to fight back? Had he called out for help? Where were his parents, anyway?

When she could see her corner ahead, she began to hope that Chad had forgotten about her. But as soon as she turned right onto her street, the breath caught in her throat.

Chad! He was waiting in a driveway behind a hedge.

In a single panicked glance, she saw Chad and Richard jump on their bikes. Fast behind them, also on bikes, came two girls from school and one girl Kate had never seen before. Only later did Kate remember that she had the same reddish brown hair as Chad and looked just as scrawny.

But while it was happening, Kate was beyond noticing which girl was Chad's sister. With a rush of energy, she veered into the center of the street, knowing the smoother pavement would allow her to go faster.

From somewhere behind, she heard Chad yell, *"Get her!"*

She pumped harder, sweat stinging her eyes. She could hear herself panting, like the sound track from a movie chase scene. A white delivery van swerved to avoid hitting her as she careened through an intersection. Turning hard out of its path, she scraped her bike pedal against the pavement. The bike skidded to a stop, throwing her sideways. She barely managed to right herself and avoid falling off, losing precious seconds in the scramble.

"Fricken' *haole*," she heard Chad say, and then another breathless voice, "Try cut her off at the corner."

She pedaled desperately as she neared the final block that separated her from home and safety. She could see her apartment building above a line of lower houses. Her lungs were burning; her thigh muscles had turned to lead.

The lobby of her building was kept locked. She prayed someone would be coming out so she wouldn't have to rummage in her backpack for keys. She never once looked around, but, toward the end, she could hear the whir of tires close behind.

She pumped harder, until she was flying down the street, houses and apartments whizzing by. Her own high-rise towered above the other buildings, looming larger and larger until she was only yards from the entrance. Without slowing down, she hit the curb, hoping to bounce over it onto the sidewalk. That's when she felt her bike lift and sail through the air. She was in free fall and knew she was going to hit hard. It seemed like forever waiting for it to happen.

She landed facedown on the cement, hands sprawled forward to break her fall. Her bike was wedged between the trunk of a palm tree and her right foot. Her palms and elbows were bleeding; she tasted blood on her tongue.

A woman who had just come out of the building knelt beside Kate just as Chad and his gang sailed by. Kate couldn't make out the words they were shouting, but she could see the scrawny girl's laughing mouth.

Later that evening Kate lay on the couch, drowsy from the pain medication the doctor had given her. All at once she had become the center of family attention, with her father, brother, and aunt all hovering around, and the TV from her father's bedroom carried into the living room especially for her.

Her father had rushed home from the office to take her to the emergency room, where he had held her hand and called her "Katey girl." Soon after they'd gotten home, Auntie Alohi arrived, bringing *lau lau*, rice, sliced turkey, roast pig, and more *haupia*. There was telephoning back and forth to report to Uncle on Kate's condition. Then, while Auntie was cleaning up after dinner,

Lopaka called David to say that he and the cousins would
be waiting for Chad when he left school the next day. It
was clear from listening to David's end of the conversation that her brother was ready to join in the fight.

Auntie put down the dishes she was carrying and
frowned over at David. "Kaleo, you tell that boy no more
pilikia. No, wait. Better I tell him!" She went over and
grabbed the phone. "Listen, son," she said, "no more
beating up! You hear me? Your uncle going school
tomorrow morning, talk to da principal. Don't worry,
mai hopohopo. We keep dis boy away from her."

Kate knew Auntie was right, but it felt good to imagine the larger cousins ambushing Chad and Richard
when they stepped out of the school yard, especially
Mario, the football player. Savoring that image, she let
her attention drift back to the TV game show.

"Uncle like talk to you," Auntie said, bringing Kate
the receiver.

"You still hurting bad?" Uncle wanted to know.

"It hurts when I laugh or cough. But it's only a
cracked rib. Nothing broken, I can still dance. They
didn't even tape it up. They just stitched the cut on my
arm."

"No worry about school. Kaleo going pick you up.
Days he get paddling, I going come get you. Let your
dad keep on study, huh?" Uncle said with a laugh. "Need
more Hawaiian lawyers, das why."

Kate hung up the phone, bewildered. Uncle had been
trying to make a joke! It was a pretty lame joke, but he'd

clearly been trying to cheer her up. And he hadn't said a thing about toughening up.

After she finished cleaning up the kitchen, Auntie brought a pill and a glass of water and eased herself down beside Kate on the edge of the couch, waiting quietly for her to swallow it.

Kate realized she'd finally learned to feel comfortable with her aunt's silence. And at almost the same instant, she surprised herself by bursting into tears. She hadn't cried once, not even when the woman was helping her up and calling her father.

"No *hilahila*," Auntie said softly, "no shame."

Kate took a breath and let it out slowly. "Why should I be so scared of them? There's not even a gang, just a couple of dumb girls who think Chad's a big shot." She wiped her tears with the back of her hand. "Chad's a little guy. Skinny, like he doesn't get enough to eat. His sister's skinny, too. I could probably beat *both of them* up! Except that I'm such a wimp. They didn't even have to touch me! I crashed my own bike running away from them."

Auntie touched her wrist. "You got no experience with beating up, with tough kids like Chad. Look where you come from. Nuns and priests and all the girls in nice sailor dresses. You ever see one fight in that school?"

"The girls had ways of being mean to each other. But never any hitting. . . . I can't understand why he hates me so much."

"He's very angry, I think. Has to blame somebody."

Kate blew her nose. "David's right. I need karate lessons instead of hula."

David came over and sat down on the coffee table, elbows on his knees. "I keep telling her she has to learn to fight back. There's a backlash against *haoles* in the schools. A lot of kids want to get even."

"So that's your solution?" Auntie said softly. "Everybody learning to fight? Pretty small island if everybody fighting everybody." She took Kate's hand. "So much hate to go around, it's hard not to hate back. Much harder than learning how to fight."

David sat scowling, like he was trying to figure out a good argument to that statement, and Auntie went to the kitchen to pack up her things. David was going to drive her home.

Before she left, Auntie brought a quilt and tucked it around Kate, then bent to kiss her. "Like gold," she said, stroking the hair away from her forehead.

"*Haole* hair," Kate said.

"From your beautiful mother. A precious gift." Auntie looked over at David, who stood waiting for her at the door. "You know why the gods made people in different colors?"

"No, why?" Kate asked.

"Too boring, everybody looking the same. The gods didn't want us to get bored." Auntie picked up her shopping bag and went out the door, closing it quietly behind her.

Just as Kate was drifting off to sleep, she realized that it was her grandmother's quilt her aunt had tucked around her, the one with the green pineapple design. Auntie must have found it in the back of her closet.

Chapter 14

The next morning Kate and her father had a meeting with Chad, Richard, Mrs. Odo, the principal, and Chad's mother. The principal, Mr. Matsumoto, announced that both boys would be serving after-school detention. He leaned toward Chad. "This thing yesterday was the last straw. Any more fighting or bullying, and you'll have to go to a special school. You stay away from this girl. No shoving, no threatening, no calling names, no nothing. Understand?"

Chad barely nodded.

"I want to hear you say you're sorry."

Chad sat staring down at the table.

"I'm waiting," Mr. Matsumoto said.

"Sorry, huh?" Chad's apology came out in a hoarse whisper. Kate couldn't look at him across the table.

Mr. Matsumoto turned to Kate's father. "Now Richard here's a different story. He's never been in trouble with the police. He likes to tease other kids—and that has to change—but, otherwise, he's stayed out of trouble."

"He's not a bad boy," Mrs. Odo said, and then, with a glance at Chad, "he just needs to find himself a better role model."

Kate's father seemed satisfied. He told Chad's mother he wouldn't go to the police to file a complaint, not unless there was another incident.

The woman winced when he said "police." She called Kate's father "sir" and promised that Kate would have nothing more to fear from her son or her daughter.

Kate felt sorry for Chad's mother. She was just as skinny as Chad and had dark circles underneath her eyes. Mehana said there were five kids at home and no father.

That morning, Mehana had noticed Kate's bandaged arm as soon as she arrived at school. "Why didn't you tell us?" she interrupted when Kate was explaining about Chad. "Rebecca could've walked you home. She knows him from way back."

"I didn't know what to do." Kate was silent a moment. "The truth is, I never had to deal with anything like Chad at my old school."

"Lucky you!"

Kate smiled at a mental picture of Chad in a quiet, orderly Saint Theresa's classroom. "Yeah, but my uncle says I need to toughen up. My brother wants me to take self-defense lessons." It was a relief to be able to talk about it, to admit the fears she'd been carrying around for so long. She felt like a weight had been lifted from her chest, and it was suddenly easier to breathe.

The hula retreat was held at a park on Oʻahu's windward coast. It started Saturday morning with a performance for some senior citizens, who were brought in on buses to the beachside community building. Kate's group danced two ancient hula and then her favorite, "Ke Awāwa." Kate had memorized the English translation, but the words sounded even better in Hawaiian. People in the audience sang along with Kumu and her ukulele band. When they got to the final chorus, several old women had tears running down their wrinkled cheeks.

Kate was in a cabin with Mehana and Rebecca, who seemed to be making a special effort to be friendly.

"No worry about Chad," Rebecca told her when they were having lunch, "he jus' like scare you." The three girls were sitting on a log, eating sandwiches and enjoying the sunshine. "I know him from kindergarten. Before his father wen' to jail. Didn't used to be so mess up. . . ." She passed Kate a package of potato chips. "Das why I always try get him settled down at school, you know."

"His father's *in jail?*"

"For drugs. Sad, yeah?"

They were watching Kumu work with one of the lead dancers from the women's group under some palm trees off to their left. The dancer would rear up on her tiptoes, lifting her arms to suggest a huge wave cresting and then rolling down toward shore. Over and over, she would do the move, and Kumu Kalama would stop her and demonstrate again.

"That's Keala," Mehana said. "She's the best. Look at how she moves her hands."

"Das why Kumu giving her one hard time," Rebecca added. "If Kumu thinks you're good, watch out." They were quiet a moment, watching the dancer, then Rebecca said, "Chad's father one *haole*, you know."

"Chad's *hapa?* Like me?" Kate suddenly remembered what Auntie Alohi had said about how difficult it was not to pass on the hate.

When Kumu called their group to practice "Ke Awāwa," she told them she wanted to see their movements perfectly synchronized. "And on the chorus, I don't want to see any thumbs flapping around like this." She demonstrated with her hands, and the girls giggled. In modern hula the fingers were held loosely together, bending only slightly as the hands sketched images of waves and waterfalls. It looked effortless when Mehana and Kumu danced, but only some of the dancers had really mastered it.

They danced on a lawn at the edge of the sand, with slanted sunlight transforming the bay into a net of diamonds. Waves lapped against the beach. The soft breeze lifted their hair as they swayed to the music, their movements blending with the ocean's ebb and flow. The green velvet mountains, jagged against the pale blue sky, seemed to look down on them approvingly. Kate felt the poetry of the song in her pores. She knew she had never danced better or enjoyed it more, not even when she performed with her ballet troupe at the Los Angeles Museum's Sunday concerts.

During their free time, Rebecca fixed Kate's hair in French braids. That night they sat around a campfire under the stars. Kumu and her husband, Uncle George, played and sang the old songs they had grown up with. Kate learned the words to the one about Queen Lili'uokalani that her relatives had been singing around Auntie's kitchen table. She also learned that Hawaiian songs often had several layers of meaning, called *kaona*, which a skilled dancer needed to be able to interpret. "When the missionaries came to these islands," Kumu explained, "they were upset by the Hawaiians' open sexuality. So the Hawaiians, out of respect, wrote songs in a kind of code." Kumu laughed. "The missionaries thought they were singing about boats and flowers, and everybody was happy."

On Sunday afternoon before they went home, the *halau* had a final meeting. Kumu talked about the march the following weekend, about how solemn an occasion it was and how important that they all behave with dignity. Their performance had to be *pono*—proper. They would all gather yellow plumeria blossoms to make their leis. Kate's group would wear *mu'umu'u* in shades of blue. Mehana had an extra one that would fit Kate.

Their group of nine-to-fourteen-year-olds would be dancing "Ke Awāwa" and one other *kahiko* hula. Then, at the end of the second day of the protest, the entire *halau* would be performing the sovereignty chant written especially for this day.

On the walls of the cafeteria, Kumu had posted charts for all the hulas showing where each dancer was supposed to stand. It was an honor to be placed in the front row. Kate was not surprised to see Mehana's name listed there for "Ke Awāwa" and her own name listed in the back row. She was not disappointed. She knew she was a good dancer. But she also knew it would take time and a lot of work to become a respected member of the *halau*.

When she got to the much larger chart for the final sovereignty hula, Kate couldn't find her name listed anywhere. She looked around, wondering who she should talk to. Mehana and Rebecca had gone back to their cabin to pack up their clothes.

"I saw you looking at the chart," Kumu said when Kate approached her.

"I couldn't find my name."

Kumu took a short breath. "I didn't put you in the sovereignty hula."

"But I know it!" Kate didn't add "perfectly," but that was true. In front of her mirror she had practiced it over and over again, every turn of the head, every undulation of the hips.

"I know you do. You're one of the best dancers in your class, at least as far as technical skill is concerned. But hula is more than just movements. . . ." Kumu sighed, and Kate looked down at her feet. "You just don't have the *mana*. And you really need it for this song. You need to *feel* the loss of our land."

Kate's eyes were filling with tears.

"Hula is rooted in the earth. The *'aina*. We get our energy from the land." Kumu reached out with her hands, groping for the right words. "In ballet the dancer is always leaping up, trying to distance herself from the earth. The two kinds of dance couldn't be more different."

"I know hula's not like ballet," Kate whispered. Her French braids were coming apart. Kate twisted a loose strand of hair until her scalp hurt. "What does it look like? For a dancer to have *mana*?"

"It's not something I can describe in words."

"Then how can I ever learn it?" Madame Briansky, Kate's ballet teacher, had been very difficult to please. But she'd always explained precisely what they needed to do to meet her standards.

"It will come," Kumu was saying. "It's not something you can work at. You just have to feel it."

Kate looked around at the other dancers—she was the only light-haired person in the room—and knew that she was never going to learn how to fit in.

It was quiet in the car going home. Her father had little to say. For the past week he'd been so busy fighting with his brother that he'd hardly seemed to notice anything else.

"You guys keep each other awake all night telling

ghost stories?" he asked at one point, as if suddenly remembering she was beside him in the front seat.

"I'm just tired." Kate turned away and closed her eyes. It wasn't fair. She was already better than Rebecca, who'd been dancing hula for years—and she was a lot more serious, more *pono*. Besides, dancing "Ke Awāwa" on the beach, Kate *had* been feeling something for the land. But she couldn't get it right, no matter how hard she tried, no matter how well she danced.

She was never going to be one of them. She was always going to have the wrong feelings or the wrong look.

Chapter 15

*A*t the last minute Kate's father was able to get an official permit for protestors to spend Saturday night camped out on the palace grounds. But that wasn't going to stop Uncle Kimo from getting hauled off to jail. Uncle wanted the permit returned to the illegal American government. The night before Saturday's protest march he came to their apartment to continue this argument. Kate and David were watching TV in the bedroom when they heard the raised voices.

Her father was yelling. "I *can't* get arrested. Lawyers aren't allowed to break the law."

"*I keep on telling you! It's not our law!*"

"Think in the long term for once in your life. I can't lose my chance to practice law in this state. . . ."

David got up from the bed and turned up the volume; the game show theme song drowned out the voices. On the screen a contestant struggled to remember the date of the Louisiana Purchase. Then the yelling got louder, and their uncle's voice surfaced.

"You still one *coconut!* Brown on da outside, white on da inside!"

"Don't ask me to choose between being Hawaiian and being American! You won't like the answer."

"Already I know! You do everything *haole* way. All you care about is *kālā*. . . . *You not my brother!*"

The slam of the front door sent the apartment walls vibrating.

"*Kālā* means 'money,'" David said. "If Dad cared about money, we wouldn't be sitting on the bed in this crummy apartment watching a crummy TV that doesn't even have a remote control. . . . I thought they were gonna hit each other this time," he added, pounding his fist on the bed.

"It scares me when they fight like that," Kate said, and then, "Do you ever miss home? California?"

"I miss Boggs. I miss the house. Remember the entertainment center in the den? We used to fight over the remote."

"Remember Mrs. Gomez's enchiladas?"

"Yeah, sure." David switched off the TV. "But even if Dad can't get along with his brother, they're still my family. This is where I belong. I never really felt that way back in California."

"How can you stand all the fighting? It makes me sick to my stomach."

Hands on his knees, David was looking down at the

floor. "It's pretty discouraging. If they can't even talk to each other, what hope is there for the Hawaiian nation?"

Kate didn't want to talk about the Hawaiian nation. "I got another letter from the Lindseys," she said. "Mrs. Lindsey says she's appalled by what happened with Chad. She wants me to come spend the summer with them at the lake. . . . I could be with Boggs."

David was staring at her thoughtfully. "That's one way to escape," he said after a while.

Later that night their father left the apartment for an urgent meeting. Kate didn't see him until the next morning, when he came back to change clothes and drive her and David to the rally. He'd already been down to the palace, where several hundred marchers had gathered that cloudy Saturday morning to listen to representatives from all the different sovereignty groups. Uncle was going to be one of the first speakers. People from HARA would be speaking later in the morning.

Kate's *halau* wouldn't be dancing until Sunday, at the very end of the rally. She still didn't know if she wanted to join them. She hadn't bothered to find plumeria blossoms to make a lei or pick up the blue *mu'umu'u* at Mehana's house. She'd spent the past week in a daze, keeping to herself at school. When Mehana found her and asked why she'd skipped Thursday's hula practice, Kate just shook her head. She couldn't find words to explain.

That morning she couldn't even decide what kind of

cereal to have for breakfast. She just stood at the counter looking out at the gray morning with the empty bowl in her hand.

"Is that what you're wearing?" her father asked, pointing with his chin at her cutoff jeans and T-shirt.

"I guess so. You want me to get dressed up?"

"Never mind. Where's David? I've got people waiting for me."

She left the house without eating anything and climbed in the car without saying a word. It was impossible to think about what she would wear, how she would fill up the hours of each day, how she was ever going to make a life for herself here in Hawai'i.

She only knew what she didn't want to do. As the three of them drove in silence down Beretania Street toward the palace, Kate knew she didn't want to be going there. She didn't want to hear her uncle Kimo's speech. She didn't want to hear any more arguments about Hawaiian sovereignty. Not one more word.

A swirling traffic jam surrounded 'Iolani Palace, set like a huge Victorian dollhouse in the middle of lush green lawns. Kate and her father got out at the side entrance; David drove off to find a parking place.

Her father was scanning the crowd. "I need to find some people from HARA," he said. "We're still trying to talk Uncle out of getting arrested. Now he wants to start a bonfire without a permit. See that bench built around a tree trunk? Let's meet there when the speeches start."

Kate went to find a water fountain. Her stomach felt

queasy; she was beginning to wish she hadn't skipped breakfast. By the time she got to the curved bench, a short, squat woman in a blue jacket was sitting there. Kate sat down and looked up at the bandstand draped with Hawaiian flags. A man was up there playing the ukulele and singing.

The woman in the blue jacket leaned toward her, frowning. "This bench for natives only," she announced. "Are you one native?"

At first Kate didn't understand the question. Then it dawned on her that the woman meant native Hawaiian, just like the Indians on the mainland wanted to be called Native Americans. *No,* Kate wanted to say, *I'm not really a "native" Hawaiian. I have no* mana, *no connection to the land.*

The woman, who looked more Chinese than Hawaiian, had short, grayish-black hair and round glasses over piercing, angry eyes. "Answer me, girl," she snapped. "You deaf or what?"

Some people on nearby beach chairs were staring over at them. *This bench is public property,* Kate yelled inwardly. *I have a right to be here!* But she couldn't make the words come out of her mouth. She finally said, "I'm part Hawaiian."

The woman's frown deepened. "*Cannot be!* If you one Hawaiian, you say it with pride, not hanging your head. And you use the proper term for our people. *Kanaka maoli.* Not the white man's name for us!" She leaned closer. "You no Hawaiian. You one scared *haole.*"

Kate got up from the bench.

"When we take back these islands, we getting rid of your kind," the woman hissed at her.

Up on the bandstand the man with the ukulele was introducing Uncle Kimo. The man told the crowd that Kimo Kahele had been kicked out of the navy because he'd refused to salute the United States flag.

Kate started to back away. People in the audience were cheering. The old lady in the blue jacket was standing up, shaking her fist and yelling, "Geeve 'um, Kimo!"

Kate turned and ran. Halfway across the lawn, she stumbled on a tree root and fell onto her hands and knees.

"You okay?" a big Hawaiian man asked, helping her to her feet.

"Fine, I'm fine." She dusted off her scraped knees.

Uncle's voice was pouring out of the loudspeakers. "My bruddah wen' get us one permit. United States government tink dey doing us one big favor. Letting us camp out on our stolen land. Just one night only. No can make noise, no can build fire. . . ."

Up on the stage Uncle paused, smiling. "I tink maybe we need one campfire for cook our food. Big one, right here. Middle of dis yard. Maybe United States police going come arrest us."

The audience roared with laughter.

Kate didn't wait to hear the rest of his speech. She turned and ran in the opposite direction—away from the blaring loudspeakers and the raised fists.

Chapter 16

Fifteen minutes later Kate was walking in the direction of their apartment when Uncle Kimo's old blue station wagon pulled up beside her. She was surprised to see Auntie Alohi in the driver's seat. She'd never seen her aunt driving before.

"Where you going?" Auntie wanted to know.

"Home. Back to California where I belong." Kate kept walking, and her aunt had to drive alongside to keep pace. "My friend Sara invited me to come spend the summer," Kate said. "Sara Lindsey. The ones who have our dog."

"Summer's three months away."

"I'll talk them into letting me come now. Mrs. Lindsey feels real bad about the thing with Chad. She's been dropping hints about me going away to boarding school with Sara next fall. Mrs. Lindsey says I could get a scholarship. Because I'm part Hawaiian and they're always looking for good minority students." Kate was thinking, *At least I can look like a native on an application.* "Or else maybe I can go live with our housekeeper, Mrs. Gomez," she said to her aunt. "My dad could give her money for my food and expenses."

She expected an argument. Instead, her aunt leaned out of the car window and asked, "You eat any breakfast, girl?"

"No."

"You should maybe eat something before you fall down. I make us pancakes back at the house." Auntie smiled. "We leave the men to argue the future of Hawai'i. For now, anyway."

Kate stood on the curb, twisting her hair. Her aunt had been very kind to her. She didn't want to hurt her feelings.

Auntie Alohi said, "There's something over there I like show you."

Kate got into the car.

Auntie Alohi wasn't much of a driver. She stalled at the first two traffic lights, mumbling *"Auwē!"*— Hawaiian for "Oh, no!" Then she had trouble getting onto the freeway. A line of cars piled up behind her because she took so long to join the traffic flow. Back in California, drivers would have been honking their horns and yelling insults. People in Hawai'i were amazingly patient about such things.

Once they got onto the highway that crossed the mountains to the windward side of the island, they drove in comfortable silence. There was little traffic, and in less than an hour they were in Auntie's yellow kitchen mixing up batter at the big center table. Kate was suddenly light-headed with hunger. The smell of frying bacon reminded her of Saturday mornings back in California.

"Your pancakes are good!" Kate told her aunt. "Even better than the ones Mrs. Gomez used to make for us."

"It's the rice flour. I teach you how to make them." They finished breakfast and then stacked the dishes in the sink and went back to the car. The thing Auntie wanted Kate to see was on the hillside above the house.

They drove up rutted mud roads past *lo'i* planted with swaying green taro. At the top of the hill Auntie parked the car, and they went to sit next to what looked like a dry streambed.

Auntie sat quietly, hands folded in her lap, her faded pink *mu'umu'u* tucked around her legs. The wind whooshed around them. Green mountains rose in sharp crags against a cloudless blue sky, giant steeples watching over the valley. It was peaceful, like being inside a church. Kate felt the knot at the base of her neck relaxing.

"The *'aina*," Auntie finally said, nodding at the terraced hillside. "It gives us our food. It holds the bones of our ancestors, and it will hold ours."

"Kumu Kalama says I don't have any feeling for the land. She thinks it shows in my dancing."

"Is that true?"

Kate shrugged. "I never thought about land back in

California. It was just something you walked on. Or paved over."

Auntie shook her head. "The land is our mother. In the old days there was no such thing as landownership here in Hawai'i. *'A'ole!* How could anyone *own* land? The *'aina* was a gift of the gods, to be cherished and protected. It owned us, not the other way around. When the *haole* came to these islands, they talked our king into letting people buy the land. Hawaiian families were supposed to make legal claims to their fishponds and taro patches. With maps and official signatures." Auntie's mouth tightened. "That's not the way it worked out. Nobody understood about 'buy.' Most people never even heard about the new laws; it took two days on horseback to get from here to Honolulu. So a lot of land was bought up by the king's *haole* advisers—the same ones who talked him into passing the laws in the first place."

"What happened to the Hawaiians?"

"They lost their taro patches and their fishponds. Many wound up as squatters on the outskirts of Honolulu. Kimo's family—your family—was lucky. Some could read and write; they got legal title to this whole hillside. All of it was planted in taro. You can still see the rock terraces. Then the government came and built a ditch—up beyond the ridge. They took our water and carried it through a tunnel in the mountains to the *haole* sugar plantations on the leeward side."

She was silent a moment, looking down at her hands.

"They took our land, then they took our water. But Hawaiians lost more than that. The *haole* took away our pride. They called us 'natives.' They told us our language was no good, that our gods were evil."

Auntie pointed to the dry streambed. "This used to be full of water, rushing down from where the mountains caught the rain clouds. It was *uluwehi*—lush—with sweet *'o'opu* fish and *'opae* shrimp. . . . After the ditch was put in, the streams dried up."

"But you have so much rain on this side of the island."

"Taro needs a constant flow of water. Too much was going over to the plantations. Your grandfather could only keep this one section cultivated. The same thing was happening to taro farmers all over the windward side. More houses coming, clearing the land. Paved roads, golf courses. More worse, now they building one superhighway! *Auwē!* That eyesore H3 spoiling our beautiful valleys, disturbing the bones of our ancestors. . . ."

Kate glanced over at her aunt. She'd never seen her get angry before.

"We gave away our land and our water—*ka wai ola*, our life source. But we forgot to tell the *haole* they should love them like we do. That the streams are our brothers. That the earth is our mother."

She was quiet for so long, Kate thought she had finished her story. Finally she continued. "When your grandfather couldn't sell enough taro to pay his taxes, he lost title to most of the hillside. The *lo'i* had been here for hundreds of years. Your grandfather felt *hilahila*—shame—that he was the one who couldn't hold on to them. He was drinking a lot, having trouble putting food on the table. . . . One night he drove his car into a telephone pole."

"He was *killed?*"

Her aunt's sad eyes answered the question. "Down there where the road curves in from the bay."

"*My father never told us!* How old was he when that happened?"

"Seven, maybe eight. We have an expression, *kāmau.* It means to take up the burden. To keep going. Kimo was only fourteen years old. The *hiapo.* But he was hardheaded, even then. Uncle took up the burden. He took care of his mother, who only lived for two more years. After that, Kimo dropped out of high school. He was determined to keep every *lo'i* his father had saved. He worked all day planting taro, all the time redesigning the water flow to take advantage of every drop. Nights he worked in the hotels."

"What was my dad doing?"

"Your father passed the entrance test and got into Kamehameha School for the seventh grade. This was a great honor for the family. Kimo made sure his brother had good clothes so no one would look down on him. Kimo worked extra hours so your father could go on school trips and take a girl to the prom. Kimo never went to a prom," she added, sighing. "Your father's college was paid for by football scholarship, but when he got into law school, Uncle paid everything. He didn't want Ikaika to have to work."

"Dad must have paid him back."

"He tried. When he got into that law firm, he offered to pay interest, too. Uncle would not accept. By that time, every conversation between them ended in a fight. You see, Uncle always expected Ikaika to come back and work for our people."

Kate stared down at the road curving in from the bay; she couldn't make out any telephone pole. "Did Uncle Kimo hate my mother?" she asked after a while.

"He didn't hate her. . . . He hated your father for wanting her, for not wanting us. For choosing to live *haole*. For not choosing the life of the land."

"But he's come back! He's selling our house. He's working at HARA for no salary!"

"A lot of them come back. Born-again Hawaiians! Some stay, some leave."

Kate thought about the chorus of "Ke Awāwa," inviting people to come back to the land—just as her father had done. "What else can my dad do to make it up to Uncle?"

"He's already given Kimo what he wanted most. Since the day you were born, Uncle's been praying for you to return to us, you and your brother."

"Uncle wants David, but he doesn't seem all that happy to have *me* around."

Auntie smiled sadly. "Now that you're here, Uncle doesn't know what to do with you. Your mother came to visit when you were a baby. . . . She was like a beautiful golden butterfly." Auntie put her hand on Kate's arm. "We didn't know how to talk to her, how to share our lives so she would understand. Uncle feels the same with you. He thinks you're ashamed of the way he talks, of the dirt under his fingernails."

Kate was about to protest, but then she realized it was true. She would have been embarrassed to bring Uncle to family night at Saint Theresa School. She wouldn't have wanted the Lindseys to see him or his battered blue station wagon.

"I wanted you to sit quietly on this hillside," her aunt said. "Our ancestors believed that when you sat on the land, or better yet, slept on it, then the dust would come into your bones. I wanted you to know you're a *keiki o ka 'aina*, a child of the land." Auntie took a short breath. "And to understand the anger between these two brothers. Kimo has inherited generations of anger. But in his heart he's a good man. And he loves you very much."

They sat there on the family hillside, listening to the birdsong and the sweep of wind in the trees. After a while Kate told her aunt about being left out of the sovereignty hula. Then she told her about the woman in the blue jacket. "Do you agree with Uncle that Hawai'i should get out of the United States for good?" she asked. "My father says people like Kimo—and that old lady at the bench—are giving sovereignty a bad name."

"I haven't made up my mind. There are more than forty different groups; all of them have plans for what kind of nation we should be." Her aunt lapsed into silence, stroking the grass underneath her hand. "But with your father and Kimo, we don't know where politics ends and family anger begins. Somehow we've got to pray that these two brothers will find a way to *ho'o maluhia*—to make peace."

"Maluhia?"

"Maluhia, peace. Your Hawaiian name, the one you'd use on most occasions. Your full name, Kama Ho'omaluhia i ka La'i, means 'child who brings peace.'" She looked over at Kate. "Hawaiians believe a baby's name should tell what that person will grow up to be. Your mother chose the names for you and your brother. Maybe she hoped you would grow up to be a peacemaker."

"I don't think I'd be very good at that."

"I know you don't want to use your Hawaiian name—your father told me what happened that first day at school—but your mother chose a beautiful name for you. She *was* trying to understand us. She knew, even when your father didn't, that he couldn't leave his past behind—or his people." Auntie's eyes had filled with tears. "I wish I could have known her," she said softly.

Driving back on the highway, Kate told her aunt she'd decided to dance the next day with the *halau* after all. "Could we stop off at Mehana's house and pick up the blue *mu'umu'u?*" she asked.

Her aunt shot her a look. "'*A'ole!* A *borrowed mu'umu'u?* For your first hula performance? At 'Iolani

Palace? With TV news cameras? We go *'awīwī,* get you your own. Nice blue island print, so Kumu Kalama be proud."

"I can't let you. I mean, I know a lot of your money goes to the sovereignty movement."

"The sovereign nation of Hawai'i is pleased to offer you your first *mu'umu'u.*"

There was a crunch of gears as Auntie downshifted and turned off the highway, heading toward Ala Moana Shopping Center.

Chapter 17

The HARA leaders managed to talk Uncle Kimo and his friends out of starting a bonfire to get arrested. More than a hundred Hawaiians peacefully occupied the palace grounds that night, her father and Kimo among them. But the brothers had found something new to fight over. Kimo's group, still determined to get national news coverage, wanted to burn an American flag at the end of Sunday's program. Kate's father was arguing that this was the wrong way to get attention.

Kate was glad to leave the warring brothers behind, and she suspected Auntie felt the same. Along with David and Lopaka, they spent a quiet night at the apartment. They ordered pizza, and David made one of his creative salads, this one with spinach, oranges, and walnuts. After dinner Auntie Alohi took up the hem of Kate's new *mu'umu'u* and helped her make leis for the next day's performance. After their trip to the mall, they'd gathered a big bag of sweet-smelling plumeria from some trees at the park.

"We make for Kumu and your friends, too," Auntie told Kate. "Come on, boys," she said, passing David a long, lei-stringing needle. "We need for the uncles, for Auntie Ruth, Tutu Kuoha. . . ."

"Why don't we just buy some leis at Safeway on our way down tomorrow morning?" David suggested with a sly grin. "You know, where they sell flowers and plants."

Auntie gave him a stern look. "'A'ole! In the old days, when Hawaiians wanted to give a gift, they didn't have Safeway. Or any money. They had to take from nature what the gods gave them. Gather the flowers, make the twine, string the flowers. Lots of time and effort. We do the work just to say, 'I love you.' No meaning when we buy a lei in the supermarket."

"Okay," David said, laughing. "Pass me some flowers. But don't complain if mine looks all *hemmejang*."

Kate's *halau* was scheduled to dance at two o'clock on Sunday afternoon, the final hula performance. She arrived early at the palace, eager to show Mehana and Rebecca her new *mu'umu'u*, a blue-and-green floral print with scoop neck and puffed sleeves. Kate liked the look of it. It was plainer, less ruffled than most of the others they'd looked at. Auntie had pulled back the sides of her hair and pinned them on top with white plumeria blossoms, letting the back hang loose. It finally grazed her shoulders and felt silky whenever she turned her head. Kate couldn't remember when she'd felt so pretty or so pampered.

She found Mehana and Rebecca practicing their hand movements, talking about how nervous they felt. Both girls seemed happy to see Kate; neither one mentioned the missed practice. Rebecca always had to go to the bathroom right before a performance, but the palace rest rooms were too far away. Mehana and Kate were laughing and telling her she should go behind some bushes, when Kumu gave the signal for them to line up with their class.

The smallest girls danced first, to the delight of the crowd. Next the boys did a hula about Hawaiian cowboys, their movements brisk and vigorous. The women's group danced a modern hula. Several TV news teams were filming—two men with cameras perched on their shoulders darting from place to place to get different angles on the dancers. Kate was afraid she wouldn't be able to ignore their presence when it was her turn.

Finally her class was announced. As she climbed the steps to the stage, she felt a fluttering inside her chest and the same numbness in her hands that she remembered from ballet performances. Silently, the dancers took their places. Then Mehana lifted her arms and sang out in a high, clear voice the beginning words to the ancient hula, a cue for the dancers. In the next instant, Kumu began the chant, accompanied by the throbbing beat of the gourds. The audience a blur, Kate concentrated on staying synchronized with the other dancers and keeping her eyes off the whirring cameras.

Before they danced "Ke Awāwa," their second hula, Kumu translated the chorus for the audience. After being with her aunt on the family hillside, Kate understood the words even better. Maybe some dust from the 'aina had come into her bones, because when she began to dance, she forgot the television cameras and let the song—and its message—move through her.

When the dancing was going well, as it was then, there always came a feeling of being at one with the music and with the whole universe. It was better than being in church.

After they left the stage, Kate noticed one of the TV photographers still filming their group. "These beautiful hula dancers represent the many ethnic groups that make up Hawai'i's population," a reporter with a beard was saying into a microphone.

The dancers had a short break before the final sovereignty chant while the same man who'd introduced Uncle Kimo the day before got up on the bandstand to thank all the march participants. He was loaded down with so many leis that they covered his entire neck and chin. Kate stood quietly with Mehana in the area behind the stage. She was still hoping Kumu might change her mind and allow her to dance the final sovereignty number. But somehow it didn't matter as much as before. If she had to write an essay to explain her absence from hula practice, she would say that she understood now what Kumu had been trying to tell her about getting energy from the land.

"Excuse me, miss, you're a very beautiful dancer," said the bearded reporter as he thrust his microphone toward Mehana. "Can you tell our audience your name?"

A photographer wheeled in and focused his camera on Mehana's face. Too terrified even to smile her shy smile, Mehana whispered her name into the microphone. The reporter had to ask her to repeat it, twice.

"Can you tell the people on the mainland what that last dance was about?" he asked.

Mehana shook her head. Kate was afraid her friend would be too tongue-tied to answer. "It's about a—uh, a valley on Moloka'i . . . where . . . uh . . . some . . . Hawaiians used to live," Mehana finally stammered.

"The song is inviting all the people to come back," Kate heard herself saying. She stepped closer to Mehana and linked arms with her. "There used to be thousands of Hawaiians living in these valleys," Kate said into the camera. "But they lost their land when the white man came. Most of them, anyway. Without the land, people lost their spirit. A lot of them caught diseases that the white man brought, and died. . . ."

A voice from behind the reporter said, "Keep her talking. Get her name."

"Is that what this rally is all about?" the reporter asked.

Mehana, with a frozen smile on her face, was clutching Kate's hand.

"Hawaiians used to have their own nation, with their own queen and two houses of Congress. Just like in

Washington, D.C.," Kate began. "But then American Marines sailed into Honolulu harbor. . . . They aimed their guns at the palace. Right here. Americans locked up the queen. . . ." Kate wished her father were around. He was so good at explaining these things, and she really didn't know all the details of the overthrow. But suddenly, instead of her father's logical speech, she heard Uncle Kimo's voice in her head. "Hawaiians never voted to be part of the United States," she said. "Their country was stolen from them one hundred years ago. That's what these people are marching about."

"Thank you for that excellent explanation. How old are you?"

"I'm twelve."

"Do all the children in Hawai'i have such an understanding of their history?"

Kate shrugged. "My father's a lawyer. He's come back here to fight for his people's land and water rights."

"Can you tell us your name?"

"Kate . . . I mean, Kathryn. Kathryn Maluhia Kahele." She scanned the crowd for her aunt. "Maluhia is my Hawaiian name," she said. "It means 'peace.'"

Chapter 18

Auntie Alohi had told Kate that spirits of the dead can visit us in dreams. That night Kate dreamed about her mother, who looked just like the photographs, with delicate hands and silver-blond hair falling across her cheek. Kate was leaning against her in the window seat, smelling the eucalyptus trees and listening to the birds. Her mother was telling her about her Hawaiian name, about why the world needs peacemakers so badly.

Kate woke up from the dream to an almost familiar smell.

"Uncle's in the kitchen making pancakes," David announced from the doorway of her room.

"Pancakes?" Kate sat up in bed.

"Taro pancakes."

"Count me out." She glanced at the clock. "It's not even seven. What's he doing here?"

"Uncle made a videotape of *you* on the late news. He

brought over Auntie Ruth's VCR for us to see. I've never seen him so stoked!" David grinned. "Come on, get up. You're a celebrity, Kathryn Maluhia Kahele!"

Kate's *halau* was on all the major networks, the camera scanning the line of dancers and then zooming in on Mehana, with Kate dancing behind her, mirroring every move. A voice-over told about the Hawaiian people, about the illegal annexation of an independent kingdom. Then there was Kate in her blue *mu'umu'u* with white flowers in her hair. Her voice clear and strong, she was explaining the message of the song, the message of sovereignty.

Looking at herself, at her face filling the screen, Kate decided she must have found the courage to speak up like that because of the rush of confidence that always came after having danced well. But her family had other ideas about her public speaking ability.

"You ought to be a lawyer," her father told her.

"One *Hawaiian* lawyer," Uncle said with pride.

For once the two brothers agreed about something.

Toward evening Kate and David were searching the refrigerator for dinner makings when their father came bursting into the apartment.

"Katey! David!" he called out. "No creative salad tonight! No Hawaiian stew! I found a restaurant that's supposed to have decent Mexican food. Stop chopping," he said, planting himself between David and the cutting board, "tonight we're celebrating!"

"What's the occasion?" David wanted to know.

"Katey's network news debut." He turned to Kate. "You've not only gotten through to a mainland audience, you've gotten through to *Uncle!* Convinced him that we don't have to burn things down or go to jail to get national attention. He won't admit it, of course. . . ." Her father came over and put his arm around her. "For years my brother's been sounding off about hula being used to exploit our people. 'Dancing for tourists in plastic skirts.' But yesterday we saw hula—our authentic culture— helping people understand what it was the Hawaiians have lost."

"Don't you have to study?" David said. "Your exam starts Wednesday."

"This is worth a couple of hours off. There's more good news. The president is supposed to be considering an official apology to the Hawaiian people. For the illegal annexation of the kingdom one hundred years ago."

"What president?" David asked.

"The president of the United States, that's what president. Go get dressed in something more formal than a T-shirt. Katey, you can wear your new *mu'umu'u*. I'll tell you all about it over dinner."

Kate's father took the bar exam the following week and felt confident he had passed. All of a sudden, he was fun to be around, actually present when you asked him a question. He and Uncle Kimo even managed to talk on the phone several times without shouting. They were making arrangements for a family ceremony, something called *ho'oponopono*, for the following weekend.

"What's a *ho'oponopono?*" Kate asked David.

"Some kind of peacemaking thing Hawaiians do. Lopaka says there's praying. And I think we're all supposed to talk about Uncle and Dad, about all the fighting. How we feel about it." He shrugged. "The two of them were pretty mellow in the car this morning. But I'm not looking forward to it."

"It's their problem," Kate murmured. "I don't see why we all have to be there." She wasn't looking forward to it, either.

When they got to Uncle's house, Auntie Alohi, Uncle Kimo, and Lopaka were sitting at the long table on the covered *lānai*. A pitcher of ice water and plastic cups were on the table, but none of the snacks Auntie always put out. Whatever *ho'oponopono* was, it was serious business. Auntie Alohi and Uncle Kimo looked like they were sitting in church waiting for the service to begin.

Auntie was in Uncle's usual place at the head of the table. Nervously, Kate sat down between her father and David. Uncle Kimo and Lopaka, who for once was not making jokes, were sitting across from them.

Looking at Kate and then at David, Auntie Alohi said, "*Ho'oponopono* means setting things right. . . ." She thought a moment and then continued. "In the old days, harmony within the family was a matter of survival. Whether they were net fishing or working in the taro patch, Hawaiians had to get along if they wanted to eat. It's like canoe paddling," she said to David. "You know how it feels—how the canoe moves through the water—when all the paddlers are of one spirit."

David nodded, and Lopaka smiled. "That's when you have *mana*," Lopaka said, "and you're winning the race!"

"But harmony—*lokahi*—is about more than winning races. It's about peace inside yourself as well as peace with others." Auntie looked carefully at Uncle Kimo and then at Kate's father. "People who are wronged are bound together with their wrongdoers. After the first hurt come layers and layers of misunderstanding. These layers need to be uncovered. That's why we're here tonight."

The ritual began with a *pule*, or prayer. Kate bowed her head as Auntie, who was clearly the leader of the event, asked God to open their hearts to one another and to the divine light that each one of them was born with.

Auntie's next prayer was in Hawaiian. Listening, Kate realized that she'd learned to love the soft, flowing vowel sounds. She wanted to study the language if she got into Kamehameha School in the fall.

"We are here to talk about the anger between these two brothers," Auntie said after a moment of silence, "and how this anger has affected our family. First we have Ikaika." She gestured at Kate's father, calling him as always by his Hawaiian name. "He went away to California. He left behind his family, his *'aina*. He wanted no part of us. Now he has come back and brought home his two *keiki*.

But his brother, Kimo, has not found it in his heart to forgive."

Kate's father was staring into the fluttering greenery that bordered the *lānai*. Uncle Kimo was concentrating on his hands, which were clenched into fists on the table.

Auntie said, "We must all share our *mana'o*, our thoughts and feelings." She glanced around, her eyes coming to rest on Uncle Kimo. "But we cannot begin unless everyone has joined in the spirit of truth."

Uncle Kimo grunted agreement. Kate barely nodded. How could she say what she was truly feeling with Uncle sitting right across from her?

After an uncomfortable silence, Auntie asked, "Who would like to begin?"

"I'll start, since mine was the original wrongdoing," Kate's father said. "I had the privilege of education. I was the first of our family to get into Kamehameha Schools. To go on to college. Instead of using this gift to care for my people and my land, I turned away from everything Hawaiian." He rubbed his forehead with his index and middle fingers. "In these islands, the *haole* held the power. I wanted to be like him. I went away to California. I didn't come back home to visit. I didn't return my brother's phone calls. After a while, he stopped calling."

He nodded at Uncle Kimo, who was still frowning down at his hands. "I apologize. And I want to make amends to my family. But I have a right to a different vision for Hawai'i than my brother's. All voices must be heard if we want to restore our nation."

A bird chirped; a car rumbled by on the dirt road. Finally Auntie said, "I agree that all voices must be heard, that we must respect one another's *mana'o*. But first there must be listening with an open heart."

Kimo raised his eyes.

"You two are locked in an anger so deep that it shuts out the rest of us," Auntie said to him. "I feel invisible when I'm around you."

David took a quick breath. "It's a bummer when you two are arguing," he said, "which is always."

"You used to be a lot of fun to be around," Lopaka told his father, "and Uncle Ikaika, I don't mean to be disrespectful, but it's like you're always trying to make my dad mad. Like everybody's happy and then you say something about HARA, and then Dad calls them a bunch of coconuts."

"I'm for sovereignty," David said. "But things get so tense, we can't even ask a question. How are we supposed to learn?"

There was another silence, then Auntie glanced at Kate. "Is that how you feel? Afraid to ask a question?"

"Always," Kate whispered. "Always afraid I'm going to say the wrong thing—like 'Hawaiians' instead of *kanaka maoli*—and get a scolding from Uncle."

She turned to face her uncle, but she was thinking of Chad. "It's not *my fault* I grew up in California," she said. "It's not my fault I don't speak Pidgin and I don't know what's going on. It wasn't my idea to come here!"

Uncle slowly lifted his head. "And I make it more hard for you, criticizing li'dat," he said so softly, his voice didn't sound like him. "I did same ting wit' my bruddah," he went on after another bout of studying his hands. "I tell him, 'Tuck in you shirt, wash you hands, do you homework.' Auntie say, 'You driving da boy away.' But I nevah listen. My bruddah Ikaika had to be one star. . . ."

Kate's father's eyes widened in surprise as Uncle continued. "People come up in da supermarket. Dey say, 'How's you bruddah, Ikaika, da football player?' I tell 'um, 'He getting ready for go law school. When he come one lawyer, he help get our water back. Take 'um to Supreme Court!'"

"I never knew you were proud of me," Kate's father said.

"I like my bruddah be perfect, 'cause I always feel so dumb," Kimo said, speaking to Kate's father as if they were the only two people in the room. "Scared da Japanese teacher going bust me for dirt under my fingernails. Scared some *haole* going laugh at me." He turned to Kate. "I so scared of your muddah," he said, "when she wen' come visit. . . . So beautiful. So good her English. Everyting perfect." He shook his head sadly. "I sound like one mean ol' buggah, but I even more scared of you."

"How can you be scared of me? I'm scared of *you!*"

Uncle shook his head again, eyes brimming with tears. "Sorry, huh? Sorry I make it so hard to be part of our 'ohana. . . ." He reached for a Kleenex and wiped his eyes. "No need speak Pidgin. Jus' stay hea with us."

"You still want to go back to California?" Auntie asked.

Kate remembered her aunt's warning about truthfulness. "I still miss Boggs. Very much. I miss my friends," she said. "But I've got some new friends, especially Mehana. And I'm starting to understand what happened here—about the land and all." She smiled at David. "I like how my brother is here in Hawai'i. He never used to have time for me back in California. I love hula and the music . . . and I love having an auntie," she said, her voice cracking as she smiled at her aunt.

Auntie Alohi got up and came to give Kate a hug and kiss.

Then Uncle Kimo stood slowly. Kate's father walked around the table and embraced him. The two big men grunted from the squeezing. There were sniffles in the background.

Even Lopaka had red, watery eyes. "Hawaiians all'a da time kissing," he said to Kate. "Gotta get used to dat."

After everyone had kissed everyone else, which *was* becoming easier for Kate, Auntie Alohi spoke about the family's strengths and blessings. The two brothers agreed that they could argue about the issues and not attack each other. In her final prayer, Auntie thanked the old gods and Iesu Kristo for helping their *'ohana* to heal.

Chapter 19

"It really happened! Look at this!" David said, coming in one morning with the newspaper, which he spread out on the table next to Kate's cereal bowl.

Kate scanned the headline: CONGRESS OFFERS HAWAIIANS APOLOGY. "Does this mean we get our land back?"

"No, but it's a start. The apology was passed by both houses of Congress and signed by the president. This puts us on much firmer ground in demanding redress."

"Redress?" Kate said, grinning. "Already you're sounding like a lawyer."

"That's not all. Look at this one! An international human rights group is coming from the Netherlands to investigate the Hawaiian sovereignty cause. They go all over the world to study the demands of native peoples who've lost their land. They'll be holding hearings. Dad'll represent HARA, arguing for a nation-within-a-nation. Uncle Kimo will be there, too; of course, he'll want *all* the islands returned from the illegal United States government."

"Oh, boy, I hope they have a good referee."

But as the two brothers planned for this international forum, the truce between them seemed to hold. At least their arguments stayed on the political issues.

The Kaheles had much to celebrate at their next family *lu'au*. Kate and David, who'd taken tests for Kamehameha School, had both received acceptance packets. Mehana was on the waiting list but had a chance of getting in for the fall semester. The best news Uncle saved until everyone was gathered at the *lānai* table.

"My niece, Maluhia," he said, smiling at Kate, "she gonna be dancing in dis year's Merrie Monarch Festival. Selected by her *kumu*. She practicing every day."

Kate felt herself beaming with pride. This statewide hula competition was held every spring on the Big Island of Hawai'i, and it was a big honor to be chosen to dance.

Uncle hadn't completely changed his personality. He was still what Auntie called "one hardheaded buggah." Hawaiians weren't supposed to brag about their accomplishments. People were supposed to be *ha'aha'a*, humble, about such things. Somehow that didn't stop Uncle from telling everyone he met that Kate would be dancing in the Merrie Monarch Festival. David's explanation was that Uncle was trying to make up for all the past criticism. Still, Kate found it embarrassing. One day after school Uncle even announced this news to the voice that took orders at a McDonald's drive-through window.

"That guy's just there to sell hamburgers!" Kate said. "Maybe he doesn't even know what Merrie Monarch *is*! He hardly even speaks English!"

"So we educate him. Immigrants gotta know about Hawaiian culture." Uncle smiled, his eyes fixed on the highway ahead. They were driving west on the freeway to a secret destination.

"I don't understand what's the big hurry," Kate said, biting into a french fry. "And what's the big mystery about where we're going?"

Uncle just shook his head.

"Does David know?"

"Kaleo get canoe regatta. Cannot come."

They pulled off the freeway and drove uphill to a large gray building with a sign that said STATE ANIMAL QUARANTINE CENTER.

"Are we adopting a dog or something?" Kate asked when they were crossing the parking lot.

Uncle Kimo didn't answer.

Kate didn't want to hurt her uncle's feelings, but she also didn't want to adopt a dog. It would be disloyal, like saying Boggs was replaceable by any old stray that happened to be available.

They entered a corridor with cages on either side. Some of the dogs were silently gazing out; others greeted them with excited barking as they passed.

Even when Kate saw him in his cage, the meaning of what was happening didn't register. She stood absolutely still, breathing in short gulps.

"Dis da one," Uncle was saying to the kennel employee who had arrived with the keys. "Name is Boggs. One fancy California dog dis girl gotta have. One Labrador retriever. Came dis morning Hawaiian Air Cargo. He one Hawaiian retriever now."

The cage door clanged open, and Boggs bounded toward them. Too well trained to jump up on people, Boggs was jumping in place at Kate's feet, his tail wagging furiously. Kate fell to her knees and buried her face in his neck. After a while she pulled away and looked into the dog's brown eyes. Would he forgive her for leaving him behind with the Lindseys?

She felt Boggs's wet tongue on her cheek. His eyes held the same trusting look she'd known since childhood. "This is your Uncle Kimo," she said, blinking back tears. "Say hello."

"Why you want one fancy purebred dog? Get plenty black dogs look li'dat," Uncle said, winking at the attendant.

Kate just smiled. "Don't worry," she said to Boggs. "Uncle Kimo's growl is worse than his bite. Go ahead, shake his hand. Look, Uncle, he still knows how to shake hands! See how smart he is. . . . Oh, thank you, Uncle Kimo!" She jumped up and threw her arms around his neck.

Kate had a hard time leaving Boggs behind. But Uncle promised that during the quarantine, she could visit every day except for her weekend on the Big Island.

David, who had plans to turn Boggs into Oʻahu's first surfing dog, would be free to drive her there most days. Uncle would see that she got there the rest of the time. He'd already made friends with the kennel attendants. One of them, the nephew of a New Nation member, had promised to take extra good care of Boggs. Even the apartment wasn't going to be a problem. In June they would be moving to a house closer to Kamehameha School.

In the car on their way to hula practice, Uncle Kimo didn't take credit for getting Boggs back from the Lindseys. Still, Kate knew he'd been the one to arrange it, to make this happen for her. "Is Sara sad about giving Boggs up?" Kate asked her uncle.

"Maybe so. But dey getting one small dog. Fluffy kind. Big dog like Boggs gotta run around. Come inside and bring mud on da white rug."

"The Lindseys don't have a white rug. They have wood floors with Oriental carpets."

"Still yet, better off with one small, fluffy *kine* dog. Pink ribbon on top its head."

Kate smiled at Uncle's image of the Lindseys' perfect dog. "You're stereotyping again," she said, and when he didn't answer, "In California some people think *you* live in grass huts."

When Uncle dropped her off at the hula *halau*, Kate ran to tell Mehana the news. The two girls had little time to talk before Kumu Kalama called up their group. In this modern hula choreographed especially for the Merrie Monarch Festival, they would be executing a complex pattern of steps, with four lines of dancers weaving in and out of one another's space. It would look impressive for the TV cameras mounted above the stage, but the movements required perfect timing.

They ran through it once, making a lot of mistakes. When the music ended, Kate heard her uncle's voice. He must have stayed around to watch.

"See? Dat one wit' blond hair?" Uncle was pointing her out to a school janitor. "One *hapa haole*...."

Blushing, Kate caught Mehana's eye.

"He's just proud of you," Mehana said. "I think he's sweet."

Kate rolled her eyes.

"She first one in our family going dance in Merrie Monarch," Uncle was saying. "Next year, she going Kamehameha School. Straight-A student. Already can do algebra. Can you believe it, little girl li'dat? Smart, yeah?"

The music started up. Mehana called out the verse, and Kate glided into the first *kaholo*, losing herself in the dance.

Author's Note

In 1993 President Clinton signed a resolution, already adopted by Congress, that apologized to native Hawaiians for the overthrow of their government on January 17, 1893, one hundred years earlier. This resolution admits that the United States Minister and US Marines intimidated the Hawaiian queen into surrendering her kingdom, which eventually became a United States territory and later, in 1959, our fiftieth state.

Today more than forty Hawaiian groups are exploring avenues toward restoration of their native rights and the return of their lands. 'Iolani Palace, former home of the ousted Queen Lili'uokalani, is occasionally the scene of peaceful protests, just as I portrayed in my novel. But the events and characters I've sketched against this historical backdrop are entirely fictitious.